INVITATION TO ADVENTURE

Invitation to Adventure

A Patrick Dawlish Mystery

John Creasey *writing as* **Gordon Ashe**

INTEGRATED MEDIA
NEW YORK

ISBN: 978-1-5040-9823-6

This edition published in 2025 by Open Road Integrated Media, Inc.
180 Maiden Lane
New York, NY 10038
www.openroadmedia.com

INVITATION TO ADVENTURE

CHAPTER ONE

LETTERS FOR DAWLISH

A very large man in a dressing-gown, fair hair on end, signed for a registered letter on the threshold of his flat in Brook Street and returned yawning to his connubial bedroom.

His wife Felicity being still asleep, the early May morning cold, he draped a bed-jacket round her shoulders and sauntered off in search of tea. The kettle on, he sat down to read his letters.

The first was from his broker. Briefly glanced through, he thrust it back in its envelope with a grimace. Several more were from house agents extolling various properties offered in response to his search for a small house in the country.

The next letter, however, appeared to be more interesting.

He read it through twice.

Dear Major Dawlish,

If I am right in thinking you are not averse to excitement—of the legitimate kind, of course—I can offer it to you. Write or telephone.

Yours very truly,

Simon G. Harcourt.

'Ho-*hum*!' said Dawlish, thoughtfully. He made the tea, put the letters on the tray and went into the bedroom. Felicity opened one eye. He began to pour out. 'Brought in for your inspection,' he said lightly, 'promises from every estate agent in the south of England offering us the one and only house which answers all our requirements.' As she sat up he handed her a cup of tea and a bundle of envelopes.

Felicity glanced through their contents, putting one or two sheets on one side, for special attention, and then, opening the last, read the letter from Simon G. Harcourt.

Her charming and attractive little face set mutinously.

'That *would* happen,' she said.

'Don't blame me,' said Dawlish hastily. 'More tea?'

'Please.' She was not smiling as she looked at him. 'Pat, what are you up to? Have you been in touch with this fellow, and arranged with him to write like this, as if it were a surprise?'

'Shame on you,' said Dawlish, virtuously. 'Simon G. is a complete stranger to me. I shall, of course, send him a formal note telling him that he is mistaken, and that all the excitement I want just now is that of looking for a house.'

'Pat,' said Felicity, taking her cup, 'look at me.' Her eyes were open wide and very direct. 'Did you arrange this with Harcourt?'

'No, no, a thousand times no,' said Dawlish.

Unbidden, there sprang up within him a sense of grievance, a feeling that Felicity was being unfair. How much of it was due to the fact that when he had opened the letter his heart had leapt and for a few wild moments he had thought of going to see Harcourt, he did not know. The one subject on which they did not see eye to eye was 'excitement'. It was not, he thought as he looked at her, knowing that his smile had become set, that he would think of doing anything foolish—it was, perhaps, the fact that if he felt inclined to take an interest in Harcourt he would not be able to do so without upsetting Felicity. In the year of their marriage, this brake on his wilder inclinations had been the one thing which, at times, stood between them.

Felicity stretched out a hand. 'I'm sorry, darling, but for an awful moment I thought you had arranged the whole thing. I don't mind so much what you do, as the thought that you think you have to trick me into agreeing with it.'

Dawlish's heart lightened as he bent forward to kiss her. 'No tricks, darling, I promise you. We'll agree to things together, or not at all. Well, what do you think of the array of desirable residences now spread before us?'

'I rather like the sound of this one,' said Felicity, picking up the top letter of a pile. 'Four Ways, Alum Village, two miles from Haslemere—'

'Which probably means two miles as the crow flies, and half-a-dozen by road,' said Dawlish grimly.

'Some furniture could be bought with the house,' went on Felicity, 'so that's an inducement. Half an acre of ground. I—Pat, what are you looking like that for?'

Dawlish was staring at the letter from Simon G. Harcourt. He turned to look at her, a faint smile on his lips.

'Haslemere and Hindhead are next door to each other,' he said, 'and Harcourt's letter is from Hindhead. To go and live on the man's doorstep would be asking too much of my self-restraint.'

Felicity said: 'We can't refuse to look at a house because of that.' Her eyes were suddenly gay. 'You could see what kind of a man he is. Yes, I know that in a way I'm contradicting everything I've said before, but you might find he's terribly bogus and putting-off, and that would simply underline my own views.'

'But supposing the opposite was the case, and the fellow's story was so attractive, that before we knew where we were we were pitched into it?'

'I like the sound of Four Ways,' said Felicity obstinately, 'and no little man from Hindhead is going to frighten me out of going to see it.'

Dawlish shrugged and turned away to bath and shave, wondering what story Harcourt would have; there was no doubt that he would hear it before the day was out, and his spirits rose accordingly. It had been his pet pretence that, although he had frequently become involved in various excitements, often helping the police and more lately working for Intelligence, he had no real desire to meddle in such matters. If that had been true, it was no longer so.

He was whistling when he went in to breakfast.

The owner of Four Ways, Alum Village, had been offered a post in India and was eager to take it. The house, however, must be disposed of first. With eager enthusiasm he showed Pat and Felicity over it. The garden, the nursery, the charmingly proportioned rooms.

'Well, now you've seen the lot,' he declared, at last. 'You'll want some time to think it over, of course, but I can't promise to hold it longer than a day or two. My wife and I have got to get to town for some frantic buying, and we're sailing next week-end.'

'Give us twenty-four hours,' said Dawlish.

'You're serious about it?'

'Oh, we're serious,' said Felicity. 'I think—'

'Twenty-four hours,' said Dawlish, firmly.

They were pressed to stay for lunch, and it was nearly half-past three before they left Four Ways in the two-seater Riley. The house was set half-way up a low hill, with sweeping views on all sides; it was a couple of hundred yards from the small, attractive village on the Godalming Road, and Haslemere itself was visible, a bare two miles away.

'Nice man,' said Dawlish. 'I think we've struck oil, my sweet.'

'What's that?' asked Felicity, abruptly.

It was a high-pitched call from behind them. The call came again.

Dawlish put on the brakes, and turned his head in time to see their host waving frantically.

'He's forgotten something, or we have,' said Dawlish. He backed the car a little, and stopped.

'There's a telephone call for you, Major Dawlish.'

'For *me*? But no one knows I've come here!'

'He certainly asked for you,' said the other.

Dawlish got out of the car and walked back to the house.

The telephone was in the hall. He picked up the receiver. There was no outward sign of surprise as he heard the speaker introduce himself as Simon Harcourt.

CHAPTER TWO

SIMON HARCOURT

'I heard you had been in Haslemere and were later reported to have gone into Four Ways, Major Dawlish. Under these circumstances, may I expect to see you?'

'I had thought of telephoning you,' said Dawlish, evasively. 'I'm afraid that—'

'I do beg you not to reject anything until you've heard what I can tell you,' pleaded the man. The voice was young, and not unattractive. 'I know it was a nerve to write to you, but—look here, can you come along and have some tea? I won't try to coerce you, and if you can't do anything, I would appreciate your advice.'

'All right, my wife and I will be there in half an hour,' said Dawlish.

He rang off, and after a few words of renewed farewell to their host, returned to Felicity, strangely unwilling to meet her eye.

There was a silence after his brief explanation; then Felicity said:

'*How* did they know where we were?'

'I've no idea.'

'They can't have watched the road for us.'

'No, but we could have been followed.'

'Surely—'

'Harcourt strikes me as a most determined young man,' said Dawlish, 'and it wouldn't be surprising if he sent someone to see us, or even went up to town himself, and watched the flat. We'll find out soon enough.'

Felicity looked pointedly ahead of her during the journey. Now and again Dawlish glanced behind him. Suspicious that they might be followed. There was no evidence to support it, however. He turned off the main road and made a wider detour than necessary.

'Enjoying yourself?' he asked, with a grin.

Felicity laughed shortly. 'I was!'

He lured her into a discussion of Four Ways until they reached the gates of The Pines. It was a large, sombre-looking building, approached by a long, winding drive, flanked by pine trees. It was a gloomy approach, holding an air of mystery and furtiveness. Felicity was looking to right and left, as if at any moment she might spot a lurking enemy. Dawlish appeared to be paying all his attention to the drive, but he too snatched glances at the lowering branches.

Yet when a man appeared, he took them completely by surprise. Dawlish jammed on the brakes and Felicity uttered a sharp exclamation. The man leapt down from the bank under the very nose of the car, brandishing something which looked like a gun. As the brakes squealed, Dawlish saw that it was a long stick, and that the man was stocky and roughly dressed. He stared fixedly at Dawlish—and then, without a word, turned and jumped back the way he had come, plunging into the dark obscurity of the trees.

'Well, I'm—' began Dawlish.

'He expected someone else,' said Felicity.

'One can only be glad that he recognised the difference in time,' said Dawlish grimly.

He let in the clutch and they finished the journey up a steep incline. The house appeared in front of them, tall, narrow, ugly, surrounded by the top-heavy pines. The garden was wild and neglected, only one small patch of ground at the side of the house appeared to be cultivated.

'I rather expected them to rush out to welcome us,' said Felicity, critically.

Dawlish took her arm and they approached the porch. The front door was closed, and in need of paint, but the brass knocker and letter-box glistened. Dawlish rang the bell. They stood in silence for a few moments, looking down at the drive. The house was on a crest, and the hill up which they had driven was surprisingly steep. They could see nothing but pine trees. Rabbits sped across the neglected lawn, a squirrel leapt from one tree to another, and disappeared.

Although the sun was bright, this place seemed dark and filled with shadows. No one answered their ring, and Dawlish rang again, then knocked.

Gradually the door opened. Through the widening gap they could see a man sitting in a wheeled chair. He looked at them with a smile, which held more than a little of youthful appeal.

'Welcome!' he said.

The effect of his appearance was startling. The brightness of his smile, by contrast, seeming to add to the gloom rather than lessen it. He was probably in the middle-twenties, dressed casually in a tweed jacket and flannel trousers.

'Come in, come in,' he said. 'Linda will be back soon, she was delayed, or she would have been here to welcome you. Shall I lead the way?' His chair, an old one, creaked as he moved with surprising speed towards an open door. They followed him into a drawing-room crowded with ugly, Victorian furniture, the heavy threadbare curtains keeping out what little light the pine trees had left.

'Linda,' went on Harcourt, 'is a cousin whose detective work helped me to find you. She goes into Haslemere most mornings, and was there when you stopped at the cafe.'

'How did she recognise me?' asked Dawlish.

Harcourt laughed lightly. 'She used to work in a Press Agency, and has often seen photographs of you. I hope that makes it sound more reasonable,' he added boyishly. He held out his hand, as Dawlish introduced Felicity. 'I'm delighted to see you both. You've given me new life—I rather expected to have no reply.'

Dawlish smiled. 'Have I such an ungracious reputation?'

'It's my speculations about you that grew to ogreish proportions,' said Harcourt. 'I see now how wrong they were!' He laughed again, but the sound was brittle and forced. 'I hope you'll forgive me for keeping you waiting until Linda returns. She discovered that we were short of milk and rushed across to the farm for some. I've been meddling in the kitchen, trying to cut some bread-and-butter. I'm not much of a hand at it, I'm afraid. As for the story, it would be as much as my life is worth to start telling you before Linda gets back!'

'We're in no hurry,' said Dawlish.

'Can I help with the bread-and-butter?' asked Felicity.

'How decent of you!' said Harcourt, with genuine feeling. 'The kitchen is really the only livable room in this morgue at the moment, and I vote we have tea in there. Follow me!'

He crossed the hall skilfully, pushing open a door with his stick. The narrow passage beyond seemed to slope; two planks had been laid down. The ends resting at the top of a high step.

'This is one of my bright ideas,' said Harcourt. 'I couldn't manage the step in the chair, and it gets lonely on one's own.' The wheels ran swiftly along the planks, gaining speed towards the far end. 'The trick is to swing into the kitchen without braking,' he declared, and with a dexterous touch of the steering gear he swung into a room on the left and disappeared.

Dawlish and Felicity exchanged glances.

'Mind over matter,' murmured Dawlish.

'He's a darling,' said Felicity.

'And in need of help,' Dawlish reminded her.

'Here we are,' said Harcourt. 'What do you think of it?'

'Charming!' said Felicity.

'I wish Linda had heard that spontaneous tribute. She did everything herself, even to putting in those tiles round the sink. See that photograph? That's Linda, bless her!'

There was pride in his voice, and there was reason for it. The girl in the photograph, dark and small-boned, was a beauty.

'She's my only cousin,' he said. 'But for her I would be—' he broke off, abruptly, and forced a smile. 'She shouldn't be long now,' he declared. 'She's been gone nearly half an hour. I hope she hasn't had a spill and dropped the milk!'

'Did she go by bicycle?' asked Dawlish.

'Yes. The farm isn't far, but it's uphill most of the way back. How I hate this place!'

In a flash, the cheerfulness was gone, the smile disappeared, and they had a glimpse of the dark forces which tormented Simon Harcourt.

Quietly Felicity began to cut bread and butter while Dawlish looked out of the window. The little patch of garden was immediately opposite, and there was other evidence that someone had tried to make the view from the window more attractive. The very attempt showed a plucky spirit, and it was easy to imagine that both Harcourt and his cousin were outstanding examples of those who strive to overcome almost insuperable difficulties.

Harcourt glanced at his watch. 'She's *very* late.' There was uneasiness in the man's voice, although he tried not to show it. Dawlish said tentatively: 'Tell me, should there be a stocky individual, wearing rough tweeds the worse for wear, lurking in the grounds?'

Harcourt gripped the arms of his chair. Felicity stopped spreading butter. There was a moment of tense silence, in which the colour drained from Harcourt's face. Then:

'Was such a one really lurking in the grounds?'

'Yes, indeed. He did more, he jumped in front of the car,' said Dawlish. 'Who is he?'

'I don't know. One of—them,' Harcourt said, with a catch in his voice. 'I don't know whether he means any harm, but—' he hesitated. 'Look here, Dawlish, will you go and meet Linda? She might—' his voice trailed off. 'If you'd rather not leave Mrs. Dawlish here, take her with you.'

'I'll stay,' said Felicity, quickly. 'You go, Pat.'

'That door leads into the garden,' said Harcourt.

As Dawlish went through it, he realised that one thing was very certain; Harcourt was afraid.

CHAPTER THREE

LINDA

The trees seemed to close in about Dawlish. The path was narrow and wound between them. Roots stuck out several inches, making it necessary to watch his step carefully; cycling down it would be a tricky business, and cycling up, at this part anyhow, literally impossible. Yet on the few patches of earth free of pine needles, he saw the marks of a bicycle tyre.

He went slowly, looking to right and left, half-expecting the stocky man to appear again. The only sound was the piping of the birds, thin and eerie, as if they also avoided this dark, sunless spot.

Presently he heard voices, a man's and a woman's.

He went forward more swiftly, the pine needles muffling the sound of his approach. Turning a bend in the path, he saw them quite clearly. The man was the one who had leapt in front of his car, and the woman was Linda.

She looked both beautiful, and exceedingly angry. She held a bottle of milk in one hand and was keeping her bicycle upright with the other; as the man's voice came gratingly:

'You'd better, or you'll have a shock one of these days. Go and tell Harcourt that—'

'We are staying!' declared Linda furiously, 'and if you don't keep away from the house I shall—I shall ask for police protection.'

'I don't think so,' said the man sneeringly. 'But don't say I haven't warned you, my pretty.' He shot out his hand, but whether to taunt, or to hit, was not clear. Dawlish, appearing suddenly between them, took it on his forearm.

'Criminal assault,' he said reprovingly.

The man glared, without speaking, out of angry, bloodshot eyes.

'Who—' he began.

'The name is—' said Dawlish.

'Don't tell him!' Linda said urgently. 'Don't tell him!' She swung round on the man. 'I warned you I would send for the police!'

'*He's* no policeman, but whoever you are'—the man turned violently—'keep clear of this woman and her fine friends—that's if you don't want to be hurt.'

'So I might be hurt,' drawled Dawlish.

'You'll find it's more than might be!'

Dawlish moved towards him, but as he did so the girl's bicycle fell in an entangled heap. Before it could be righted, the man disappeared among the trees.

'I'm awfully sorry,' Linda said. 'I—'

'You mustn't lie to me,' said Dawlish, reproachfully. 'You didn't want me to catch him, did you?'

She stared at him, her green eyes bright with alarm, or mortification, or else with a fear which she had not fully conquered. For a moment he thought she was going to deny the accusation. Instead, she raised a hand helplessly.

'No, not yet.'

'I hope you've a good reason,' said Dawlish.

'I—yes, I've a good reason,' she said. 'He hasn't *done* anything but talk, yet, but he might get vicious if you try to browbeat him and then go away and leave us here on our own.' As if to avoid his eyes, she bent down to the bicycle.

'Let me,' said Dawlish. He lifted the machine with ease, and they started to walk back to the house. 'That's a good point,' he admitted, 'except that if I started anything I wouldn't leave it to anyone else to finish.'

She bit her lip.

'I—I hope you will help us, but I couldn't be sure, and Simon can do nothing. I'm not a lot of use,' she added bitterly. 'Has Simon told you anything?'

'No, he was waiting for you.'

She smiled appeasingly.

'I thought it would be better if I were there. He might gloss over some parts of it, not thinking them important, and I believe you should hear everything, as you have been good enough to come. Did he ask you to meet me?'

'He was getting a little worried about you, although he didn't say so in so many words.'

'Everything went wrong,' she said.

'That happens sometimes.'

She said passionately: 'How I hate this place!'

He made no comment, remembering that Harcourt had said much the same thing.

They walked on in silence. Dawlish had the impression that she was frightened, as Harcourt was, but that something was making them stick this place out. They had written to him as a last resort, a despairing effort to get help because—and this was obvious—they could not go to the police. Dawlish was, in the main, suspicious of people who were reluctant to go to the authorities, but that made little difference to his estimate of Linda and her cousin. Here were all the signs of a long, stiff battle which gripped both his imagination and, in a smaller extent, his compassion.

They were in sight of the kitchen window when Linda stopped, and faced him.

'Major Dawlish, will you help Simon? We're not asking you to take risks just to save our own skins. It's deeper than that.' She caught her breath. 'You can see how helpless Simon is. He is paralysed from the waist downwards. He was a lieutenant with the glider-troops, and crashed. He—oh, he deserves all the help you or anyone else can give him. I don't think there is another man living who is so brave.' She gripped his arm. 'Will you promise to help him?'

'Promises are tricky things, blind ones even more so,' said Dawlish sombrely, 'but if I see a reasonable chance, and the motive doesn't frighten me off, I will try.'

'What do you mean, frighten you off? You're not afraid of danger, are you?'

'Our ideas of what is legitimate might not coincide,' Dawlish said lightly.

'Oh, if that's all, there isn't anything to worry about,' said Linda. 'Ah, here we are.'

They had reached the kitchen.

After a formal introduction Linda appeared to withdraw into herself. Now and again she looked at Harcourt; that she was desperately in love with the man was glaringly obvious. Harcourt was in great form. He chatted gaily of this and that; but presently there was a lull.

It was as if a blanket of depression had been dropped over his head and Linda's. There were a few moments of silence while Linda poured out tea, and then Harcourt straightened up in his chair and said abruptly:

'I give you my word, Dawlish, that if I weren't tied to this chair I would not have written to you. It's the helplessness which is so damnable. I inherited this house about six months ago. It seemed like a dream come true. My first glimpse of the place was certainly a little depressing, but we would have got on all right had we been left to ourselves. I ought to explain,' he added, 'that Linda gave up her job and came down here to look after me when she realised that it would be some years before I could look after myself. The only alternative was a home for the disabled. I didn't fancy that. I would be sunk without Linda.'

'Don't twist a pleasure into a duty,' said Linda, laughing. 'It'll turn both of us into crosses for the other to bear.'

Harcourt smiled a little grimly. 'The fact is, Dawlish, that I have no close relatives except Linda and her brother. I've lost touch with my friends, and in any case I couldn't go begging for help.'

'Well, we came here and Linda started to put this room right, and I busied myself with some writing. For the first three months all went well, and then the man whom you saw outside met Linda in the grounds one day, and told her we must go. Just like that—he didn't explain, just told her to be out within a week. We decided he was a bit funny in the head. Even when he did the same thing the following week and the week after that, we didn't really take him seriously.'

'I see,' said Dawlish, when Harcourt paused.

'The next thing was when I went into Haslemere one day—I can just get this contraption up the drive, with Linda's help,' he added, patting the side of his chair, 'and while I was in the High Street a well-dressed, rather pompous chap came up to me and asked me to sell him The Pines. He offered a fair price, and said he understood I was selling. I told him he was mistaken. He persisted, and in the end I had to be pretty sharp with him. Next morning I had a letter. He more or less ordered me to sell him the house, and said that if I were still here in a week's time his offer would be halved. I ignored it. He wrote again, quoting half the original offer.'

'Did he give you an address?' asked Dawlish.

'No—he told me to meet him in Haslemere at a certain time, to close the deal. I didn't turn up. However, Linda insisted on going. He was very much the same with her as he had been with me—affable at first, and then vaguely threatening. The next night we had visitors—of a kind.'

'Burglars?' asked Dawlish, lightly.

'Nothing so simple! Two men knocked at the front door and said they had come to take possession! They had a car outside, and a reservation at a local hotel for us both! They pretended not to believe me when I said that I hadn't sold the house, and they were a long time arguing. Finally they went off, and it was from that night onwards that the man whom you saw has haunted the grounds.'

'But why didn't you carry out your threat and contact the police?' Dawlish asked mildly.

'I did,' said Harcourt. 'I asked them to come and see me. A sergeant from Haslemere turned up, a nice enough fellow, heard my story, and promised to have the house watched. There was a policeman on duty for a week, and during that time nothing happened. After that, naturally, the police took their man off, and asked me to let them know if there was any more trouble. However, the next step was a letter. It was pretty potent, and threatened serious injury to Linda if I went to the police again. It—er—'

He broke off, in some confusion.

Here, thought Dawlish, was the reason why Linda had been

so determined to be present when the story was told. Harcourt was keeping something back, and she did not intend to allow that.

She said quickly: 'It contained a threat to my brother.'

'Lin, you needn't—'

'If Major Dawlish is going to help us he must know all the facts,' said Linda, 'and I am not going to allow sentiment to stand in the way. Barry, my brother, is rather younger than I am, Major Dawlish—in fact, he is twenty-two. In many ways he is a young fool. I don't know how he got mixed up with these people, but I do know he became involved in some crime. The letter said that if we persevered with the police, it would mean a prison sentence for him.'

'What has he done?' asked Dawlish.

'I don't know. Immediately after getting the letter I went to London and saw him. He admitted that these people *could* do him great harm, but wouldn't say what particular thing he had done. He was thoroughly miserable and frightened, and I rather think he is still being coerced into working with them, or for them.'

Dawlish nodded. 'Have you still got the letters?'

'That's one of the rubs,' said Harcourt ruefully. 'I had them all together, locked up in a desk, but three nights ago they were stolen. That leaves us without any evidence at all.'

'And that's the lot?' asked Dawlish.

'I daresay it sounds pretty thin to you,' said Harcourt, a little wildly, 'but I don't mind admitting that it has got on my nerves. Apart from everything else, I'm afraid to let Linda go out of the house, for fear of what might happen to her.'

'I can appreciate that,' said Dawlish, 'but people don't do violence lightly, you know—the bigger the crook the less likely he is to commit grievous bodily harm. It looks as if they are concentrating on frightening you out of the house, and that brings us to the obvious question—why?'

'I haven't the slightest idea,' said Harcourt, helplessly.

'The man gave you no guide?'

'None at all. As a matter of fact, I *have* a theory,' went on Harcourt, 'but it's probably pretty wild, and I've no real grounds for it. This piece of ground, twelve acres in all, is sandwiched between two other pieces already being developed in a fairly well-to-do way. I've had several letters from estate agents, asking me whether I'm prepared to sell, and offering fairly good prices. I suppose you're going to say that the sensible thing would be to do just that, and get out.'

'Some people would say so,' said Dawlish.

'It would be the most sensible solution,' said Harcourt miserably, 'but I don't like being frightened away, and in any case, Barry's in trouble. I thought if we could find out more about the people who are trying to scare us, we might help him. In any case, if it's just that the land is wanted for building development, why should Smith be so eager to get us out at such short notice?'

'That's a point,' said Dawlish. 'There's really nothing else you can tell me?'

Harcourt shook his head. 'I know it must sound a trivial business to you, compared with some of your cases, but it *does* matter to us, and life is pretty well unbearable. Will you—er—do you think you might—er—'

'I think I might,' said Dawlish, smiling. 'Don't get the notion that I'm a second Sherlock Holmes, Harcourt—I'm an amateur, I blunder, I bluster, and sometimes I'm lucky. Also, I have friends. Could you put up with one or two men staying here as guests? In fact—' his eyes were suddenly bright, and he snapped his fingers. 'That's an idea. Put an advertisement in the local paper, asking for paying guests. Those who answer it might well be worth looking into, and of course there'll be the one or two friends of mine I'll send along. Well, what about it?'

Harcourt looked excitedly at Linda. Her eyes were glistening. 'It's brilliant!'

'It certainly has prospects,' said Dawlish. 'But don't count too much on them. The best we can say is that it's worth trying.' He sat back in his chair, then shot forward suddenly, looking at Felicity. 'If we were invited to stay here for a few days, while the applicants for board-residence come along, would you say yes? It'll be convenient for visiting Four Ways, and—'

'Yes,' said Felicity, a little sadly.

'Simon,' said Dawlish with a sudden, broad grin. 'Your stars foretell some unexpected guests!'

CHAPTER FOUR

INVITATION FOR TWO

Dawlish left, on his own, half an hour later. He was going to London to pack some clothes, and planned to be back by about nine o'clock. Felicity had no objection to staying at The Pines, and Dawlish saw no reason to believe that the danger would be any more acute that evening than it had been for the last week.

As far as he could tell, he was not watched or followed on any part of the journey, and he reached the Brook Street flat a little after six o'clock. He packed three cases, after consulting a list which Felicity had written down for him, and then telephoned the Carilon Club, where he asked for Mr. Beresford or Mr. Jeremy.

Beresford's powerful voice soon came on the line.

'Did I hear aright?'

'This is no time for joking,' said Dawlish. 'I—'

'That is the very thing I am afraid of,' said Beresford, bitterly. 'Here am I with the prospect of a pleasant evening of joviality and merrymaking before me, playing billiards on and off with Tim, which you—if I mistake not—are proposing to shatter!'

'Billiards can be played any night of the week,' said Dawlish ruminatively. 'But a punch on the nose—'

'What is that alluring remark you have just dropped? A punch on the nose? May I inquire if it is to be given, or received?'

'I rather thought that would be up to you.'

'Oh, you did, did you. Sounds interesting. On the whole I think you might expect both me and Tim—'

There were few men Dawlish would as readily choose to have with him in a tight corner. All three of them had weathered many a storm together, Dawlish as their chief counsellor and guide. All were quick-witted, but Dawlish possessed that extra touch of acumen which made him, almost automatically, their leader.

In the Brook Street flat, once assembled, they spread themselves in easy chairs, tankards of beer to hand.

'I'm leaving again before eight,' said Dawlish, 'so I haven't much time. Here is the situation.' He took far less time than Harcourt had done, yet when he had finished they knew all that it was necessary for them to know. Beresford finished a tankard with great relish, while Tim Jeremy raised one eyebrow.

'You do find them out, don't you?'

'They found me out,' said Dawlish. 'Now, for opinions. I don't know the man or the girl well yet, but I'm inclined to accept their story. I think it's possible that there is something which they haven't yet told me about, but I doubt whether it's of much consequence. One thing is certain; they are badly worried. Linda is desperately in love with Harcourt, while he, whatever his affections, is certainly not the type of man to saddle a girl with a helpless cripple.'

'Major Dawlish, the well-known romantic,' murmured Jeremy.

'The relations of these two people might have more importance than we can yet see,' said Dawlish. 'Their lives together, in such restricted circumstances, demand a degree of familiarity which has all the ingredients for an emotional storm or two. In any case, on the girl's side the atmosphere is tense enough. Both have guts; both are determined to see the extraordinary persecution through, though Harcourt admits that the sensible thing would be to sell the place and get out. So the thing they may not have told us is why they're determined to stay there, and why they sent for me. I wouldn't be surprised to get a visit from the suave gentleman, telling me his side of the story.'

'Or dotting you one,' said Beresford.

'So far there is no indication of violence,' said Dawlish, 'and I don't think they'll resort to it just yet. Well, now—our position is this. They're going to advertise for paying guests in the local paper, and you two will answer it and take up residence there. Felicity and I will give the other applicants a once over as they come—we might pick up something that way.'

'Hum,' said Beresford.

'The next thing is this erring young brother, Barry Keen. I would like you to find out what you can about him. The girl gave me his address—Wickham Mansions, Maida Vale. He has a small flat, and enough income to make work unnecessary, or at least unacceptable. I must say he sounds a highly unsatisfactory brother to me, but we won't jump to conclusions. Keep an eye on him, won't you?'

'Anything else?'

'If you could persuade him to come across with the names of the people with whom he is working, it would help,' said Dawlish, 'but don't press him too far. Try to meet him casually, find out all you can about him, but don't let him know that you are really acting as agents for his sister.'

'We can count up to six,' said Jeremy, reprovingly.

'How was I to know?' demanded Dawlish. 'I thought three was your limit. Oh, by the way, just in case of accidents, you'd better have a gun apiece when you come down to Surrey. Any more beer?'

They left at half-past seven, and Dawlish had just finished his packing when the telephone rang. The familiar voice of Superintendent Trivett boomed down the line. There was nothing strange in receiving a call from Trivett; the strangeness lay in the timing.

Dawlish's greeting—carried almost to the point of garrulity—coming to an end at last, Trivett spoke again.

'Splendid! Now if we've finished with the courtesies, Pat, let me get a word in. Are you particularly busy just now?'

'Busy!' exclaimed Dawlish. 'My dear chap, I'm frantically overworked, running hither, thither, and yon, after a house. Yes, that's what I *said*. A house. You would never believe the job it is. We spend day after day toiling through murky mausoleums, each murkier than the last. This morning we hit the first possibility. Felicity is still down there, grimly waiting for the hordes of bloated profiteers she's convinced are about to offer twice as much as the place is worth and three times as much as we can afford. Take my advice, old man—'

'Now tell me what you're really doing,' said Trivett patiently.

'But I *am* telling you!'

There was a slight pause, and then Trivett said:

'So Felicity and you are thinking of buying The Pines, at Hindhead.'

There were some moments, Dawlish admitted, when he was completely stymied, and that was one. He uttered a plaintive exclamation, and fell silent. There was a chuckle from the other end of the line, and Trivett went on:

'I'll give you a quarter of an hour to get over the shock,

Pat, and then you may expect me at the flat. You never know, you might prove helpful.'

Dawlish replaced the receiver, looking rather dazed. Then picked it up again and put through a call to The Pines. Linda answered him, and he asked if he could speak to his wife.

Felicity, when she came, assured him that all was well, and nothing out of the ordinary had happened.

'Excellent, as far as it goes,' said Dawlish. 'My news may be a little more startling. Trivett knows something about Harcourt and the girl. I can't tell you what. He's coming to see me, and will be here in a few minutes. Find out whether they know that I know Trivett, and whether they realise that Scotland Yard is interested. All clear?'

'Yes,' said Felicity, doubtfully.

'I'll be back sometime tonight unless I ring again,' Dawlish added.

He replaced the receiver in time to greet the Superintendent as he came up the stairs.

Trivett was a man whom most people instinctively liked, and he was popular at the Yard. They had been friends for seven years. It was a friendship which had made many difficulties for Trivett, who did not always find it easy to defend Dawlish's unorthodox methods of action.

'Have a drink,' invited Dawlish, hospitably.

'No, thanks,' said Trivett with a smile.

'Which means that you are on business.'

Trivett shrugged. 'Where are Tim and Ted?'

'Not under the sofa at the moment. I take it you have had the place watched?'

'I wanted to find out whether you were up to anything,' said Trivett blandly, 'and I did. How on earth you manage to get mixed up in these things I just don't know. Do you smell them out?'

'The other way round would, in this instance, be more accurate. I was appealed to.'

'You mean that Harcourt sent for you?'

'Just that,' said Dawlish simply. 'Now, what's it all about?'

'The devil of it is, I don't know,' said Trivett. 'The only fact I'm sure of is that I was at Guildford a few weeks ago, and there was a little trouble at The Pines. I wouldn't have been interested, except that the stocky fellow Harcourt mentioned answered the description of a man in whom we're very interested. They put a sergeant on to watch the house, and when nothing happened in a week, he was officially removed. Unofficially the place is still under surveillance, and you were seen to go there this afternoon. Haslemere Police told Guildford, the central authority in that part of Surrey, and Guildford, knowing that you and I are acquainted, thought I would like to know.'

'So it was as simple as that,' said Dawlish.

'Harcourt gave our people the impression that there was something he was keeping back,' said Trivett. 'What did he tell you that he didn't tell us?'

'He told me precious little, except that the police were apparently inactive, and he was still being pestered to sell the house,' said Dawlish. 'But for the fact that Fel and I were looking at a house near The Pines, I doubt whether I would have gone to see the chap. Are you being frank? Is that all you know?'

'Yes—except that this well-dressed, rather flashy-looking fellow who wants to buy the house has been buying up a lot of property. Still, there's nothing illegal about that—I haven't any evidence that he's used pressure before. We're interested in him for a very different reason. Did Harcourt tell you about his cousin Barry?'

Dawlish said: 'Barry?' He sounded almost too innocent, and Trivett grinned sardonically.

'Barry Keen appears to be a foolish young man who has got himself mixed up with a dubious set of people led, as far as I can find out, by the flashy man—'

'Could he have a name?' asked Dawlish hopefully.

'The only name we know him by is Bland,' said Trivett, 'but the initials on his cigarette case are "A.L.", so your guess is as good as mine. We don't know anything against the fellow, except that he has a number of acquaintances who are sometimes on the wrong side of the law.'

'Meaning jailbirds?'

'Some of them are. Others have been suspected and watched, but always managed to keep clear of trouble. Don't get the idea that we're seriously worried about Bland and his friends—we haven't got beyond the stage of being interested in them. We thought we might get something useful from Harcourt—'

'Don't you consider threats of violence useful?'

'Certainly, if the threats can be substantiated. They haven't been yet. There were letters, but these, Harcourt says, were stolen. Offers to buy a man's house, even if couched in dictatorial terms, don't constitute a crime. The question is,' went on Trivett, 'whether you're going to try to help Harcourt, and if so, will you keep us informed of what happens?'

'Very cunningly put,' said Dawlish. 'I suppose I can't say "no" although I'm not at all sure that I am going to help him.'

Trivett smiled broadly.

'The words may be doubtful, but the meaning is clear enough!'

'Maybe,' said Dawlish, smiling. 'In any case I'm reserving judgment. If Harcourt is up to anything that will bring them in conflict with the police, I shall advise him to tell the whole story. If it's something where I might be able to help him without making it official—' he shrugged his shoulders. 'Your move.'

'Fair enough,' said Trivett. 'As a matter of fact, Pat, I wanted only to find out how far you'd gone, and tell you what I knew. I don't think you'd be crazy enough to take part in anything criminal, but Harcourt's physical disability is a pretty good puller of heart-strings, and we all have our soft spots, some, admittedly, more soft than others. Well, after that cryptic remark, I'll away to do some work.'

Dawlish watched from the window as Trivett entered his car. The smile of farewell, still lingering on his lips, stiffened suddenly as he noticed a stationary car wait for Trivett's departure, then pull up outside his own house. He caught a glimpse of a rather portly man as the car door opened. After a short wait, the front door bell rang.

Standing on the threshold, smiling broadly, was a well fed—perhaps over-fed—man of undoubted good looks. Everything about him shone—his jewelled cuff links, his hair, his shoes, his nails, even his teeth and his eager blue eyes—all radiated a calculated brightness.

He leaned forward confidently.

'Good evening, Major. I hope you will forgive this unheralded call, but if you will allow me a few minutes of your valuable time, on a matter of some urgency, I shall be more than grateful.'

With a neat flourish he handed Dawlish a card. Without very much surprise Dawlish saw that the name inscribed on it was:

ALGERNON L. BLAND
THE 'Q' CLUB.

CHAPTER FIVE

MR. BLAND GIVES A WARNING

Within the flat Dawlish and Algernon Bland faced each other.

'I am delighted to meet you, Major Dawlish. Your name and your deeds of heroism have been blazoned across the headlines of our newspapers for many years; and there can be few who are not familiar with your photograph.'

'You exaggerate,' said Dawlish coldly.

'I assure you that I do not, sir. I repeat, I am proud to know you. Accept these words, Major Dawlish, as my most sincere tribute to you, and through you to those countless nameless heroes who have made this country free!'

At first, as Bland's fulsome phrases boomed through the room, Dawlish felt nauseated, then genuinely surprised, for this man was serious.

'Nice of you,' murmured Dawlish.

'Believe me, sir, I appreciate your modesty. No man of your renown likes it to be said so boldly that he is what he is. However, I look upon it both as a duty and a pleasure to call a brave man a brave man. And now you will be curious as to the purpose of my visit. You probably guess that I did not come *only* to express my appreciation of your services to our wonderful country.' He looked roguish. 'Mind you, Major Dawlish, I would consider myself justified in coming with that purpose only in mind. If I went out without another word, I would consider my time well spent. However, there are other matters. It is easy to talk of heroism, easy to say that a man has done his duty by his country and deserves well of it. Seeing that he *does* well is a different matter.' Bland took out a fat, gold cigarette case, with the letters A.L. formed in diamonds. It was not surprising that everyone who had seen that cigarette case remembered the initials; even Dawlish could hardly take his eyes off it. If the jewels were genuine, and he thought they were, it was worth at least five thousand pounds.

'Will you accept a cigarette, Major Dawlish?'

'I prefer a pipe,' said Dawlish.

'Ah! In your case an epicurian taste indeed! But now to business, Major Dawlish! Why have I come?' He leaned forward, earnestly, and his voice dropped almost to a whisper. 'I have come, my dear sir, to perpetuate the debt which I, as a citizen of this country, owe to you and such men as you; to offer you a post which is not onerous, and the duties of which might well be described as light, but which is undoubtedly remunerative. In short, I consider that *you*, of all people, have earned some reward for your labours. Will you accept, Major Dawlish, a position on the board of my company.'

Dawlish allowed himself a look of calculated surprise.

'You are astonished,' said Bland. 'You think perhaps that you may not have the agility of mind to cope with the intricacies of high finance. I wish to put your fears entirely at rest there. The post which I offer you carries with it a salary of five thousand pounds a year! That is a handsome sum, but it need not be all, Major Dawlish. Mine is a parent company. There are others and there will be more. You may, if you so desire, spring from afflu-ence to affluence. However, for a start—one post, one salary. Well, Major Dawlish!' His beam was so expansive that Dawlish could see the glittering fillings of his shining teeth.

'You are extremely good,' murmured Dawlish.

'Nonsense, sir, nonsense! You have earned it! You will, perhaps, wish to know what company I control. That is natural. I have brought with me some papers which you can study at your leisure. I can also offer you the names of some of the highest in the land, Major Dawlish, the highest in the land, as references. They will assure you of my goodwill, my reputation, my integ-rity. I seek only to serve!'

'I would like to look through the papers,' murmured Dawlish.

'As I said, sir, at your leisure. I should add one word of warning. For reasons which you will readily understand and which I need not elaborate, I wish to fill the vacant position on the board without delay. It is now Wednesday—may I ask for a decision by Friday?'

'Certainly,' said Dawlish.

'A thousand thanks, Major Dawlish! May I say how much I appreciate the kindness which has prompted you to listen to me, a complete stranger? I am enthusiastic, I admit it, determined at all costs to make sure that you have your just rewards. You are a married man, I believe, Major Dawlish.'

Dawlish nodded.

'So I understand. How delighted your wife will be when you find that you can afford, perhaps more readily than you had ever hoped, to heap the glittering ornaments of this world upon her. It is an added pleasure for me to realise that I can assist in this, which I believe is your earnest desire. Oh! one other thing! In the event, the unlikely event I am sure, of any distressing accident occuring to you, what a relief it will be for you to realise that *she* need not want!'

'Why should I meet with an accident?' asked Dawlish.

'My dear sir!' Bland looked distressed. He leaned forward and gripped Dawlish's hand in both of his; they were warm and soft, the skin silky. 'Do not misunderstand me. Accidents are the concomitancy of progressive civilisation! You will be the first to admit that. I cannot, too strongly, deplore them—in fact when I have time I propose to turn my attention to the problem of brightening the lot of those many brave, resolute women who have become widowed by accidents. But my dear Major! Why are we talking so dolefully!' He took out a gold watch, as diamond-studded as the cigarette case, and stared at it in alarm.

'My dear sir! I have taken up more than half an hour of your time! Forgive me!' He rose majestically to his feet, one hand outstretched. 'Major Dawlish, this meeting has been a great privilege. I am refreshed indeed. I give you my word, it has been a delightful encounter. I shall look forward to seeing you on our board. I shall value your suggestions and criticisms. We need fresh blood! Believe me, we need fresh blood!'

He was at the front door before Dawlish could catch up with him. He opened it, put on his hat with a flourish, raised a hand, and then went downstairs with a firm, steady tread.

Dawlish stood gazing after him. So great was the effect of the man's words that he was late in getting to the window, and he had time only to see him drive away.

'We need fresh blood,' mused Dawlish. 'Hmm. Mine, forsooth.'

Driving back to The Pines, he admitted to himself that Bland's visit had been disturbing. In spite of the blandishments and the verbiage, there was something about the man which impressed him, a note of strength, confidence, and determination. He had come with a set purpose, and believed he had achieved it. The envelope of papers he had left, Dawlish had thrust unopened in his pocket, for time was running short if he hoped to complete his journey before dusk. He was still several miles from Godalming, however, when the bright lights of oncoming cars began to appear.

It was quite dark when he reached The Pines.

The gates were closed, and he had to get out to open them. He could hear nothing but the smooth ticking of the car's engine— and yet he felt on edge. The lurking menace in those oppressive trees seemed greater. Shadows seemed darker. He had a feeling that if he could turn the light on to them, he would see men standing, absolutely still, watching him.

From the very beginning, he had the uneasy feeling that he was being watched, and yet he had found no evidence of it.

Bland's words kept recurring: '*We want fresh blood.*' Odd that the man's flowery speech had left such an impression upon him. He had not been at ease from the moment Bland had left the flat.

The house showed up, stark and uninviting. The brightness of the headlamps outshone any light that might be coming from the window. He switched them off. He saw then that the windows cowered back like unlit caverns. He switched on the headlights again, and brought the car to a standstill.

He pressed the horn; the low-pitched note made him start, in spite of knowing that it would come. The note faded, but there was no move, no sound, no sign that the house was occupied.

Then suddenly a voice came from the side of the car. It was a soft, mocking voice, one he had never heard before.

'*Go on, Major Dawlish. Don't be afraid. Go on.*'

CHAPTER SIX

THE SILENT HOUSE

Dawlish sat quite still.

He did not even turn his head; he wanted to make the speaker think that he had not been heard, wanted to tempt him to come forward, so that he could be seen. The voice came again.

'Go on, Major Dawlish, go on—your wife is in there.'

Dawlish pushed the door open and flung himself out of the car. By the glow from the headlights he saw the figure of a man disappearing among the trees. He leapt forward, but all he heard was a low, mocking laugh. He stood quite still on the edge of the trees, peering into the darkness, hearing no other sound. Silence enfolded him. He turned, with an effort of will—and then he heard the crack of a shot. The bullet struck the headlamp, which went out; the tinkling and cracking of breaking glass disturbed the quiet, and then stopped. A second shot struck the further lamp; now only the dim sidelights glowed.

Dawlish thrust his right hand deep into his pocket, feeling the cold steel of an automatic. It should have given him confidence, but it did not. He took a step forward, half afraid that the marksman would shoot again; but nothing happened. He switched off the sidelights, and the darkness was complete. A sudden gust of wind sprang up as if from nowhere, stirring the trees and bushes, with a soft, sighing sound. That faded. He walked forward slowly, heading for the porch, fighting down an almost superstitious fear. He pressed the bell.

There was no answer.

He pressed again, keeping his finger on the bell-push; nothing happened, nor could he hear the bell ringing. He took his finger away, and seized the knocker, thundered on it, risking the fact that the sound made him an easy target. The heavy banging seemed to go on and on, fading only after a long time. No one answered the door.

He turned the gun in his hand and brought the butt heavily against the coloured glass of the door panels. The crash echoed high, glass falling on the floor of the hall, but when it had stopped there was no further sound. He groped inside for the handle, turned it, and pushed the door wide. Now he was in the hall, but there was still no sound or sign of movement, and there was no light. He lit a match and saw that the electric switch was by the drawing-room door. He reached and pressed it; nothing happened.

In the flickering light, he saw that the bulb had been removed.

He entered the drawing room, but here the same thing happened. He struck another match. The curtains were drawn, and there were the embers of a wood fire in the large, old-fashioned grate. He bent down and put his hand near them; they were warm.

He moved towards the kitchen, making his way carefully down the runway which Harcourt had invented.

He struck another match, hoping to find a lamp; there was none. He moved on into the wash-house and here, for the first time, luck was with him. Feeling along shelves and ledges, every ounce of his perception centred in his fingers, he came upon a rolled-up packet of candles. The discovery put new spirit into him.

There was no wind, and the flames burnt steadily as he placed them in key positions about the house.

He hardly knew what he felt.

Anxiety; dread for Felicity; Bland's cry: '*I want new blood!*' 'Go on, Major Dawlish, go on—your wife is in there.' The words echoed with his footsteps as he went from room to room, but all on the first floor were empty. There was a secondary staircase, but the rooms above were all unused and unfurnished. Cobwebs hung in corners and at windows as if no one had lived in them for a long time.

The desolation, the emptiness of the house, filled him with a reasonless, atavistic instinct to flee from it; but not before he had found Felicity. He had not yet fully searched the ground floor, and his heart beat fast as he hurried down the stairs.

There were two pantries, he remembered, both near the kitchen. They were his last hope. He opened the first door; shelves, a sink, and some preserving jars were all he saw. He stood outside the next pantry, his hand unsteady on the handle. Then he flung it open.

No one was there.

Something glistened in a corner. He went nearer, and saw a heap of electric light bulbs. The plug above his head was bare; he put in a bulb, then switched on the light; he was dazzled by the glare.

Determinedly, trying to get his thoughts in order, he went from lighting point to point, putting in the bulbs and switching on. The house was soon a blaze of light. He realised that there was no longer any sense in trying to search by himself; the grounds would have to be combed, and the police were needed.

As he stood there, working out his next move, his eye lighted on an, as yet, unsearched cupboard in the shadow of the stairs. He strode towards it and tugged at the handle; but it was locked.

He took out a penknife, opened a blade, and worked at the lock. It was not difficult to manipulate, and presently it clicked back. Hardly daring to hope, filled with fear of what he might find, he opened the door—

They were there, all three of them, Felicity, Harcourt, and Linda. Their arms were bound, and gags covered their mouths.

CHAPTER SEVEN

WARNING

They had been put there before dark; three men had entered the house by the front door and surprised them in the kitchen. They had not been roughly handled, and the bonds, although secure, were not unduly tight. There was nothing savage about the way they had been gagged. Stiff and not a little frightened, there was now a brittle gaiety, born of relief, in all of them. Over hot tea and a snack meal they began to talk almost garrulously of their ordeal, each giving widely different descriptions of the men who had attacked them.

At last, Harcourt said:

'Well, we've spent enough time on saying what happened—does anyone know *why*?'

'Scare motive,' said Dawlish. 'Warning of what is to come if you persist in staying here. I don't think there's much doubt about that, and I'll say this for them,' he added, 'they had me scared. Still, we should be all right for a day or two now.'

'I can't see why,' said Linda. Relief had brought a lessening of the tension which had possessed her earlier in the day.

'Well, having warned us, they're likely to give us at least

twenty-four hours to act on the warning. Tomorrow we shall probably get another letter from your Mr. Smith, with peremptory instructions. I wonder what they'll do when they see the advertisement,' Dawlish added with a grin.

'You're incredibly matter-of-fact about it,' said Linda.

Dawlish smiled.

'The best way to accept these johnnies, and really the biggest snub they could get. Let's forget the business as much as we can. I've not been inactive, and my friends are coming along to help—they'll be here officially in answer to the advertisement, of course.' He gave them descriptions of Beresford and Jeremy, but he did not mention Trivett or the visit from Algernon L. Bland. He wanted to talk first to Felicity, but after the excitement he expected Harcourt and Linda to make a late night of it. It was Harcourt who began to yawn. Now that the stimulus of rescue was over, he looked pale, as if it had taken a lot out of him.

Linda was quick to see it, and rising with quiet, nurse-like professionalism, helped him from the room.

Dawlish and Felicity remained silent and alone.

Depression and shock had left their marks on her, and Dawlish wondered anxiously how far he was justified in putting her to the strain of the, perhaps, greater risks to come. His more recent adventures had been directly to do with his work for Intelligence; this was not, and there was not the remotest likelihood of him being directed by his office to work on it.

'I suppose,' he said, tentatively, 'we should have stayed away.'

She stared at him in astonishment.

'*Away?*—after what we know?'

'But—'

'No "buts",' said Felicity firmly. 'Call me inconsistent and changeable if you like, but tied up in that foul cupboard I sensed something of what this means to Simon. If he were a fit man, if he had not crashed, he would have flung himself wholeheartedly into the fray, now he is eating his heart out because of his help-lessness. Linda realises it, that's why she is fighting. We *must* see them through. You will, Pat, won't you?'

'If putting him right with himself is dependent on putting the whole thing to rights, then we'll go to it,' said Dawlish.

She gave him a brief and friendly kiss, as if sealing a bond.

'Right. Now tell me what Trivett had to say.'

'Nothing compared with what Bland had to say when he called on me after Trivett had gone,' said Dawlish. He was still telling her when Linda came back, to announce that Simon was already in bed. After a moment of rather strained silence, she said abruptly:

'Mr. Dawlish—save him for me.'

She turned away, not waiting for an answer, taking refuge in the usual hostess chatter of hot-water bottles, extra pillows, and plans for their comfort.

Alone at last, after testing the mattress and altering the tilt of the dressing-table mirror, Felicity turned to Dawlish. 'Tell me more about Bland,' she said simply.

'I told you about his flattery, his semi-disguised threats, his need—and believe it or not I can't get the words out of my mind—for new blood,' said Dawlish slowly. 'But there must be something more behind the man's colossal vanity than that.'

'What kind of something?'

'Well—supposing he is going round to men who have won medals, and asking them to act as guinea pigs on his company or companies? A V.C. has pulling power, you know. Publicity value. And a man who *seems* to be exerting himself to acknowl-edge their war service would gain some public support.'

'Aren't you going a bit too far?'

'Probably,' said Dawlish, moodily. 'It was an idea, that's all. That reminds me. I haven't looked at the papers he gave me. Throw it over, will you? It's in my wallet.'

He arranged himself in bed, then opened the envelope.

After an appreciable silence, Felicity said: 'Found anything?'

'An apparent clue,' said Dawlish. 'The company is the Merrick Estate Company Limited. Housing contractors and general builders. New shares are being issued, but there's nothing surprising in that. It has government authority, and according to the list, a number of useful contracts. It has all the appearance of being a genuine, going concern—and on its board of directors there are three men, each holders of the Victoria Cross.'

Felicity said, with a catch in her breath:

'Pat, you're uncanny.'

'Not really,' said Dawlish. 'It was an association of ideas. I had a very strong impression that what Bland said to me he had said before. It was an easy step from there to seeing a possible reason for it. This is a job for Trivett.' He tucked the papers away and switched off the light.

A letter came by the first post, which reached The Pines a little after eight o'clock. There was nothing for Harcourt or Linda, only a typewritten one for Dawlish. He opened it, being fairly sure what he would find. It was even more brief than he had expected.

'You cannot wish to invite trouble. Tell Harcourt to sell, and leave him. The house must be empty by Saturday afternoon.'

'That gives us a day or two,' said Dawlish, aloud.

'What gives us a day or two?' asked Felicity, suddenly coming from the kitchen. 'Breakfast is ready—what's that, the post?'

'Yes, as expected,' said Dawlish. He showed her the note, and added. 'We mustn't forget to see Four Ways again today, we don't want to lose that place—or have you had second thoughts?'

'I think we ought to go over this morning,' said Felicity.

'We could telephone.'

'There's no reason why we shouldn't go out for an hour,' said Felicity. 'It isn't likely that we'll have any trouble until Saturday afternoon.'

'That's so,' said Dawlish. 'Even my acceptance or otherwise of Bland's offer can wait till then. If I accept,' he added thoughtfully. 'I might be able to find out something by sitting on the board. I'll have a word with Bill about that.' He kissed her forehead, unexpectedly. 'What's for breakfast?'

'Bacon and eggs.'

'Lead on,' urged Dawlish, 'it would be a pity to let them get cold!'

He showed the others the letter, but they were not unduly disturbed.

'You don't know what a relief it is to have you here,' Simon confided.

'Ah, well, here I am in spirit—and in body, most of the time. At the moment we have to go out for an hour or so—can we give either of you a lift into Haslemere?'

'A little difficult for me,' said Harcourt, 'but Linda will like the chance, I expect. I can't understand the woman,' he added with a grin. 'Every morning she disappears about half-past nine, and doesn't get back much before lunch-time. I think she has a secret passion.'

'If you can describe the W.V.S. as a secret passion, and take "every morning" as being only four mornings a week.' Linda spoke lightly, but there was an edge to her voice, and her colour was high. Harcourt appeared not to notice that, however, and waved them off in a mood of rather forced good humour.

Dawlish dropped Linda at the W.V.S. office in Haslemere, then drove on.

'I'm going to take the car into a garage to get the headlamps repaired,' he told Felicity. 'Slip back and see where Linda goes, will you?'

Felicity shot him a startled glance, but as he pulled up outside a garage, she walked back the way they had come. An alert-looking man in overalls greeted Dawlish, who pointed out the damage to the headlamps. He saw the man's face change, and met a sharp, inquiring gaze.

'How did that happen, sir?'

'I was shot at,' said Dawlish, briefly. 'Keep it under your hat until this afternoon, will you?'

He left the man gaping. Whether he would keep silent for a few hours was doubtful; Dawlish decided to telephone the police from Four Ways. He sauntered along the High Street, where Felicity quickly joined him.

'You'll never stop surprising me,' she said, a little crossly. 'I thought you were crazy, but she—'

'Left the W.V.S. shop and went along to *Surrey Studios, Ltd. Photographers*,' said Dawlish with a grin. 'No, my sweet, don't stand in the middle of Haslemere with your mouth open. You'll have everyone looking at us. Shall we walk to Four Ways, or hire a car?'

'Let's walk.'

Once they had started, she turned on him. 'Now, perhaps you will unravel the mystery.'

'No mystery really, or if there is, a very simple unravelling. Linda has given up her work in a Fleet Street photographic agency, The Pines menage is in obvious need of money. What more natural than she should take up a similar job, saving Simon's pride by keeping it dark.'

Felicity looked straight ahead of her.

'Sounds simple when one hears the explanation. The only thing is, you saw it and I didn't!'

Dawlish squeezed her hand. 'It happens to be my job.'

Felicity said sombrely: 'Not so much your job, as your dearest love.'

'Why deny it? Would not a lie be more cruel than acceptance?'

They walked on, unconsciously soothed by the glory of the day. As they came within sight of the church tower Dawlish glanced at his watch.

'Half-an-hour exactly,' he said. 'Not bad going.'

They reached Four Ways, a little shocked and put out to see a Lanchester outside, with a chauffeur standing at the door.

'I hope we haven't lost it,' said Felicity nervously.

'I don't believe they'll sell it over our heads,' said Dawlish. He looked hard at the Lanchester. 'I think I recognise that car.'

'Who owns it?'

'Who else,' said Dawlish heavily, 'but the man who wants to make the country fit for heroes to live in?'

CHAPTER EIGHT

MR. BLAND BIDS HIGH

'Let's go in unannounced,' Dawlish said.

They could hear voices when they reached the hall, but the sitting-room door was closed and the words were not distinguishable. Dawlish glanced back over his shoulder. The chauffeur was moving from the car towards the window.

'He's going to warn his boss,' said Dawlish, and gave the sitting-room door a loud tap, opened it, and stepped in breezily. 'Anyone about? I—oh, I *am* sorry!'

The Owens turned to look at him, and he thought their expression was one of relief. Bland was standing facing them. His expression was one of astonishment and something less definable, before he stepped forward with both hands extended.

'My dear Major Dawlish! What an astonishing coincidence! I can hardly believe my ears, I really cannot! Is this your charming wife?' He seized Felicity's hands. 'My dear Mrs. Dawlish, let me express my great pleasure at this most fortunate encounter! Major, don't tell me you learned I was here and hurried to tell me that you have accepted my offer? It is the kind of thing which one might expect from such a man as you, but—*is* that what happened?'

'No,' said Dawlish, smiling. 'I came to buy a house.'

'You came to—You came to buy *this* house?'

'Certainly,' said Dawlish.

'I told you—' began Owen.

'Mr. Owen told me that he had given someone an option,' said Bland, earnestly, 'but I did not dream it was you. Major Dawlish, I know that I am taking further advantage of your generosity, but I hope—I hope very much indeed—that you have not set your heart on Four Ways. Belle, my wife, has fallen in love with it. I even went so far as to offer Mr. Owen fifty per cent *more* than he had already been offered. I do hope that we shall not fall out over it, Major Dawlish.'

'We—' began Dawlish.

'It is a most embarrassing position, *most*. If it were anything but this particular house, this dream residence, which will make Belle so happy, I would retire gracefully from the scene. In fact I would even advance you the money to meet the higher price which, I am sure, Mr. Owen will insist on getting now that the offer has been made. I do hope you will understand that my insistence, my inability to withdraw, is not a personal issue between us. I only wish I could see a way in which we could circumvent these most awkward circumstances. I do, most assuredly.'

Dawlish said: 'My wife likes the house too.'

'How distressing!' exclaimed Bland. 'If only—'

'But we can't afford your price,' said Dawlish, almost casually, 'so that settles the deal, I'm afraid. I'm sorry that your wife and you don't see eye to eye, Mr. Bland.'

Bland was startled. 'I don't quite understand you.'

'It's easy enough to understand,' said Dawlish. 'If she were at one with you in wanting to make sure that those of us who have so splendidly done our duty were rewarded, I'm sure she would withdraw her interest in Four Ways. Perhaps at a later date you'll be able to convert her to your generous way of thinking.'

Bland gulped.

'I do assure you, Major Dawlish, that this grieves me—it really does. But a man's first duty is to his wife and family.' There was a slight pause. 'You will agree, I am sure. I cannot disappoint my wife.'

'But she hasn't seen it!' cried Mrs. Owen.

'I *know* that she would be terribly disappointed and deeply hurt if I were to lose such a gem as this,' said Bland. 'Major Dawlish, I beg you not to take umbrage. Mr. Owen is a business man who understands the value of money, and—'

'Would rather like a say in the disposal of his house,' Owen completed for him tartly. 'I told you when you came, Mr. Bland, that there was an option on the house until three o'clock this afternoon, and if Major Dawlish wishes to take the option, the house is his.'

Bland was dumbfounded. 'My dear sir! Three thousand pounds *more* than you expected is not a sum which you can cast aside. It is no trifle. It—'

'Doesn't interest me,' said Owen curtly.

'What an astonishing man!' exclaimed Bland. 'I have never, in all my life, met a man who was prepared to ignore in so cavalier a fashion an offer of such value. Come, sir! Think! Consider your duty to your wife.'

'I am of the same opinion as my husband,' said Mrs. Owen.

'It—it is unbelievable,' said Bland. 'Major Dawlish—you understand my circumstances, I am sure. My wife is a determined woman. I admit that if I go back to her and tell her that I have failed, she will not only be deeply hurt but she will think that I have failed her. That is not a pleasant conclusion for a wife to reach. May I ask you to withdraw your offer, out of the kindness of your heart, and allow me to buy the house?'

'I've never heard anything like this,' said Owen. 'Can't you take no for an answer, Mr. Bland?'

'In my experience, everything is attainable, given the necessary determination,' said Bland, 'and in this case—' he looked at Dawlish, and his voice dropped. 'Major Dawlish, I am quite serious. I wish to buy this house. Yesterday it was my very great pleasure to make you an offer which I should be most reluctant to withdraw. However—'

'So you weren't sincere,' said Dawlish, dryly. 'That's a pity. Still, we're going to accept Mr. Owen's most generous gesture— don't you agree, Fel?'

'I don't like making them lose—' began Felicity.

'Exactly!' exclaimed Bland. 'Your wife is right, Major Dawlish! She would feel conscience-stricken if she did anything which meant the loss of such a sum of money to these very charming people who, out of a mistaken sense of gallantry, are prepared to stand that loss. Let us talk no more about it.' He delved into his pocket and drew out a cheque-book. 'I will pay you half of the money *now*, Mr. Owen, and the balance on the completion of the purchase. Is that satisfactory?'

Owen said: 'If I'd wanted ten thousand for the house, I would have asked for it. If you offered me twice that amount, and Dawlish withdrew his offer, I wouldn't sell it to you.' He stepped to the door. 'Good morning, Mr. Bland.'

Bland stared at him.

He opened his lips to speak, then changed his mind, his gaze turning slowly to Dawlish. He waited. Dawlish looked out of the window.

Bland said: 'I shall expect to hear from you, Major Dawlish. I shall be at my club for the whole of this afternoon.'

He strode out.

Before the front door had closed behind him the engine of his car started up.

'Peculiar chap,' Dawlish observed casually.

'I can think of stronger descriptions,' exclaimed Owen. 'But Dawlish, what—'

'It's a very long story,' said Dawlish, 'too long to weary you with, as you're leaving England so soon. To summarise, both Bland and I are interested in a little mystery which centres at Hindhead. He would rather I chose a house further afield.'

Owen's expression suddenly cleared.

'So you're *that* Dawlish! I'd no idea! I—darling, don't you realise who it is? Pat Dawlish, the—'

Dawlish smiled a little shyly. 'I'm always nervous when I meet someone who has heard of me. There are two sides to a penny, and heaven knows how many more to a man. All of mine feel very guilty now, at being the cause of you losing three thousand pounds.'

Owen laughed. 'Nonsense! If it's a help towards dotting that gentleman one, it's cheap at the price.'

'Are you sure you're right to oppose him?' suggested Mrs. Owen. 'He looked to me as if he could be very dangerous.'

'I think he is,' said Dawlish, 'but danger can be a challenge, one my wife will tell you I find difficult to resist. That reminds me, may I use your telephone?'

He put in a call to the Haslemere Police and learned that the garage man had reported the bullet-shattered headlamps. He was relieved when the Superintendent added:

'I had a call from the Yard, Major Dawlish—they told me not to be too surprised if I heard from you. You are helping them, I believe.'

'I'm trying to,' said Dawlish, fervently grateful to Trivett. 'I don't like poaching on your preserves, but—'

'I shouldn't worry too much about that,' said the Super-intendent, 'but I would like a word with you in person, when you can arrange it.'

Dawlish replaced the receiver with a certain amount of relief, and went back into the sitting-room. Felicity and Mrs. Owen were discussing curtains. Owen suggested a walk in the garden, which they had not yet seen, and strolled ahead with Dawlish.

'I don't know just what you're up to,' he said, 'but we shall be here until tomorrow, and we could stretch a point and stay over the week-end. Can I help at all?'

'I don't think so,' said Dawlish. 'But it would be a great concession if we could come in and out here, next week. It's asking rather a lot, I know, but—'

'Nonsense! We shall have packed what we want to pack by tomorrow, and you may as well take it over as a going concern. I'm asking a brother of mine to arrange to sell off the oddments you're not taking, but there's no hurry—I'll leave you his address, and you can get in touch with him when you're ready.'

'You're very trusting,' murmured Dawlish.

Owen laughed. 'I wasn't joking when I said I realised who you were! Only too glad to help.'

Taking leave of the Owens, Dawlish and Felicity set out briskly for The Pines. At the gate they met Linda hurrying back from her supposed visit to the W.V.S.

Dawlish began to feel uneasy. He had taken it for granted that nothing would be done by Bland until Saturday, when his armistice expired, but Bland might have read into the battle for Four Ways the answer to his ultimatum, and decided on quick action against Simon Harcourt. It was a relief to see Harcourt sitting outside the kitchen window, tapping away at a typewriter swung over his knees on an invalid table.

'Hallo, everyone,' he said, cheerfully. 'Everything under control, the casserole in the oven and potatoes in the steamer.'

As soon as the women had moved on to the kitchen, Harcourt's expression changed.

'Dawlish, did Linda go to the W.V.S.?'

'Why, yes, she—'

'Oh, she probably got out of the car there,' said Harcourt abruptly, 'but I've an idea that she is working somewhere.'

Dawlish said, gently.

'Supposing she does do a job? She did in London, didn't she? It's no different from that.'

'It's a lot different,' said Harcourt. 'I wasn't an expense then. She just won't stop getting specialists to examine me, and is working her fingers to the bone. If there were only a way out of this place without surrendering, I'd take it like a shot.'

'And for ever afterwards reproach yourself,' said Dawlish. 'Look here, my friends are coming down and you may decide to pick one or two of the other people who apply for apartments here—it could be made a profit-making business, couldn't it? A kind of small private hotel.'

'With Linda doing all the work!'

'You'd have to get some staff.'

'Anyhow, I can't charge *your* friends.'

'Now don't be silly,' said Dawlish. 'If I'd thought it wiser, they would have gone to a hotel and paid pretty heavily. Talk to Linda about it.'

'She wouldn't listen,' said Harcourt.

Dawlish smiled. 'Two stubborn people! If you've got the idea that Felicity and I—and our friends—are doing this as a Sir Galahad act, get rid of it. You're very wrong, you know. It's meat and drink to us. Apart from that, Bland is a dangerous customer. You are probably only one of the victims. This is one little part of the whole show, and *you're* performing the service by giving us a chance of tackling Bland. You've already contributed a lot by holding out for so long. Supposing you'd done what most people would have done—sold out as soon as he made you the offer? We would have been back at square one.'

'I suppose there is something in that,' said Harcourt.

'There's a lot in it. And I can tell you that the police are more than interested in Bland. I don't propose to tell Linda, because it might add to her worry about her brother, so keep it under your hat.'

Harcourt's surprise was so genuine, so unalarmed, that Dawlish gave up, once and for all, the thought that he might have a secondary reason for wanting to avoid the police. 'I'd no idea. You—' A loud shout cut him short. It came from the drive, and Dawlish swung round in astonishment, recognising the voice. There, standing on the drive and violently beckoning was Beresford, a Beresford, tousled and untidy, with twigs and leaves sticking to clothes and hair. He beckoned again, and then disappeared in the trees.

'Who on earth—' began Harcourt.

'That's one of my warriors,' Dawlish said. 'I'll be back.' He hurried down the drive, his hand in his pocket, wrapped about his gun.

CHAPTER NINE

BARRY KEEN

'What is it?' Dawlish asked, briefly.

'Young Keen,' said Beresford. 'He left his flat in a hurry and came this way. A bunch of thugs followed him, and we followed the thugs. Tim's about somewhere, trying to head them off.'

'Where's Keen?'

'Somewhere in the woods,' said Beresford, 'scared out of his wits. They're after his blood, all right.'

'How many are in the hunt?'

'Three, at least.'

'They shouldn't be hard to handle,' said Dawlish. 'Haven't you any idea what part of the wood Keen is in?'

'No, not really. He would choose a place like this,' he added with a touch of bitterness. 'What with the trees, ditches, and folds in the ground, they can hide for a day without being seen.'

'So can Keen,' said Dawlish, dryly.

They made their way cautiously forward. Both men made little sound; they were helped by the carpet of pine needles, and were well trained in the craft of moving silently. Suddenly, there came the crack of a shot.

'Left!' whispered Dawlish.

'A rifle,' said Beresford. 'Not Tim's automatic.' They made their way cautiously towards the left. Dawlish had no idea how far the trees stretched; they seemed interminable. Five minutes passed without an incident, and then the crack of the rifle was repeated. It was still from their left, and they edged towards it. Here the trees thinned to a clearing, in the centre of which was a dip. As they drew nearer, a third shot came. A bullet ricocheted and was lost in the earth not many feet in front of Dawlish.

'Stay here, Ted,' he said. 'Watch for the flashes.'

Dawlish slipped back into the cover of the trees, deciding to approach the clearing from a different angle. Suddenly he caught sight of the head and shoulders of a man lying in the dip. Two more shots rang out. One bullet struck the ridge within a few inches of the bowed head.

Swift upon it came the sharper bark of Beresford's automatic. The shot brought two in reply, both fired aimlessly into the trees, and unlikely to do much damage.

Dawlish was wondering why Jeremy was so silent. There was a chance that he had been hit. For the rest, it seemed clear enough that the man in the dip was Barry Keen, and his assailants were trying to pick him off. Dawlish wasted no time in speculating on the daring of the attack. He did wonder whether it would not have been wiser to telephone for the police. Wiser, perhaps, but not nearly so exciting, for there was no gainsaying the extraordinary sense of satisfaction and exhilaration that had gripped him.

He edged towards the far side. Beresford fired again, and this time brought no responding shot. The fellow in the dip lay so still that Dawlish began to wonder whether he had been seriously injured. He set that fear aside, as he caught sight at last of the first of the assailants. There was a fallen trunk of a tree, rotting with age, and the man was taking shelter behind it. He fixed again; almost simultaneously there came an answering shot from Beresford. The man ducked; pieces of bark flew off the tree.

There should be three men. Dawlish worked further behind the sharp-shooter, and then saw the other two. One was slumped forward, his head bandaged. The third man was moving away from him, gun in hand.

By the side of the injured man was a sawn-off rifle.

The uninjured sharp-shooter joined his companion behind the tree, the third man was left on his own. So they must be feeling fairly confident that they would not be taken from the rear.

Dawlish drew within a few yards of his quarry without being seen. Lunging forward he knocked him out with a swift and economical blow. It was no time for squeamishness. Then, picking up the gun he moved on. The two sharp-shooters were still firing spasmodically at Keen.

Suddenly Dawlish saw the emerging figure of Tim Jeremy, covering the couple with his automatic. One man sprang to his feet, while Dawlish, wasting no time in words, went forward and swung the shortened rifle; the crack of the butt on the man's skull sounded loud. The second man had a moment's warning, saw that the situation was hopeless, and tried to rush between them. Tim stretched out a leg and tripped him, following up the man's fall with a blow on the side of the head.

'Is that the lot of 'em?' asked Dawlish.

'All who have crept out of the wood-work so far,' drawled Jeremy. 'Nice show, Pat!'

Dawlish sprang towards the dip, alarmed because the figure there had not stirred. He called out: 'All safe, young fellow!'

There was no response.

Dawlish went down on his knees and, attempted to lift him.

There was blood on his left side, a little below the shoulder. The pale face, the open mouth, alarmed him.

'How bad is he?' asked Beresford tersely.

'Bad enough,' said Dawlish. He rolled a handkerchief into a tight pad and pressed it gently against the bullet-hole, attaching it with a strip torn from the shirt. Then, gently, he raised Keen in his arms.

Two of the men were now conscious, and on their feet. Beresford was lifting the third. Dawlish led the way, finding the drive after ten minutes. Near the house he could see Felicity and Linda following Harcourt's wheeled chair.

He waved reassuringly, calling: 'All safe, barring a few minor injuries! Linda, hop back and telephone for the doctor, will you? Tell him an ambulance might be needed.'

'Who's hurt?' asked Harcourt.

'I don't know,' lied Dawlish.

Linda did not hesitate. Felicity came forward. As Harcourt caught sight of the man in Dawlish's arms his face blanched.

'Dawlish, that's—'

'I know,' said Dawlish, compassionately. 'I thought we'd gain a few minutes for Linda. Will you tell her, or shall we?'

Harcourt stared at the pale face.

'It will be a terrible shock to her.'

'I'll tell her,' said Felicity, decisively.

Before either of the others could speak, she ran back to the house. By then they were joined by Beresford and Jeremy, Beresford still carrying one man, the others being herded along by the threat of Jeremy's gun.

Dawlish, glancing behind the little cavalcade, saw an agitated policeman wheeling his bicycle up the drive.

Harcourt neatly intercepted him, allowing the others to continue their way towards the house.

Linda met them, white-faced but calm.

'Take him to Simon's room. I'll get some things.' She turned back to the kitchen while Dawlish lowered Keen on to Harcourt's bed.

He wished that he could make sure of being with Keen when he recovered consciousness, but he was too badly hurt to rely on first-aid; as soon as the doctor arrived, he would have to be moved to hospital.

Dawlish stood aside as Linda and Felicity took charge of the wounded man. Linda had obviously had medical training and worked swiftly and competently. There was nothing further that Dawlish could do. He knew that there was an even chance that Keen would die. If he did, all their effort had been wasted, and there would be no chance of learning anything from him. At least there were the prisoners, but even with them there was little hope of being able to question them himself, for the police would soon be here in strength. They would not allow him to break regulations, and unorthodox questioning would be impossible.

Harcourt was coming along the kitchen passage, talking to the constable. Apparently he had satisfied the man that there was no need for alarm, and as soon as he reached the hall, he said:

'There's the telephone, Constable.'

'Thank you, sir.'

Dawlish looked at the two conscious prisoners. *Was* it worth trying to slip in a few hurried questions before the police came?

Beresford was standing by the window, and Dawlish beckoned to him.

'Get outside. If one of them makes a run for it, give him some rope, but don't let him get far,' he whispered.

Beresford's ugly face broke into a smile, and he hurried out.

Dawlish turned towards the injured man, his back towards the others. The policeman came into the room, importantly.

'Tim—' began Dawlish.

As Jeremy turned his head, one of the two made a rush for the window. Jeremy swung round, raising his gun; Dawlish knocked it aside, as if by accident.

'After him!' roared Dawlish. 'Front door, Tim!'

He himself rushed to the window, and collided with the policeman. Beresford was just in sight. The escaping man did not glance behind him, but sped towards the trees. Jeremy came into sight from the side of the house, running to catch him off. Beresford would tell him what the game was, Dawlish knew; there was a risk that their quarry would escape, but it was worth taking, and he felt more at ease as he backed away from the window, apologising profusely to the indignant policeman, who with some difficulty lumbered after the others.

In the hall, Harcourt was sitting with his forehead wrinkled, a thunderous scowl on his face. He looked at Dawlish, and then turned his head away.

'If I could only get at the blighters—'

'We will, in time,' said Dawlish, 'and we haven't done so badly. Two prisoners for the police and one, with a bit of luck, for us— you'll be able to try your hand at third degree!'

'Did you *let* him go?'

Dawlish shrugged his shoulders with an illuminating grin.

'How is Barry? My sympathies are so much with him and his sister.'

Harcourt's eyes flashed. 'For Linda, yes, but as for Barry—' He broke off abruptly, for Linda was coming out of the downstairs bedroom. She was pale, but she looked less harassed than she had been, and her first words brought relief to Dawlish.

'I think we'll be able to save him.' She glanced out of the doorway, and her face cleared. 'Here's the doctor, and—but who's with him?' she added, her voice rising. 'I don't recognise them, do you, Simon?'

CHAPTER TEN

FRIENDLY NEIGHBOURS

Dawlish's first thought was that the police had come with the doctor. One was a tall, lean fellow of about sixty, a man of some breeding and with a high opinion of himself, Dawlish thought, the other, younger and less austere, could not have been more than thirty.

'I hope you'll forgive us worrying you, Mr. Harcourt,' said the older man. 'We both heard the shooting, and were rather alarmed. We met at the gate and the doctor came along and offered us a lift up the drive. I trust that no one is badly hurt.'

Harcourt answered with a brusqueness verging on hostility, 'It's extremely good of you to inquire.' He turned to Dawlish. 'Allow me to present Sir Raymond Graham and Mr. Perry Lamb—my nearest neighbours. Major Dawlish.'

Graham was looking at Dawlish, with a faintly patronising air, while Lamb's glance swept searchingly about him.

'I say, Harcourt, I hope it isn't your cousin who is hurt!'

'Miss Keen is perfectly well,' said Harcourt frigidly.

'So that's how the land lies,' thought Dawlish.

'That's splendid!' said Lamb. 'I—why, there she is!' He hurried along the hall to meet Linda. 'Here I am to see if I can help, Miss Keen! Please make use of me!'

'My brother has been hurt,' said Linda, smiling a little.

'Oh, I *am* sorry.'

Dawlish was wondering why she had not recognised him in the car. True, they had been sitting at the back, but there was no suggestion now that they were strangers, and he wondered whether Linda had, indeed, recognised them, but in deference to Simon's prejudice, pretended not to. It was going to be difficult to get at the whole truth while there were these undercurrents of emotion.

'Forgive me, if I rush away,' Linda murmured, 'but I'm on an errand to the kitchen.' She hurried off, while Dawlish wondered what Harcourt would do next. It was decided for him by the arrival of the police. He was sure they would understand, he said, if he did not entertain them, and Dawlish grinned to himself when he saw Graham's cold expression, and the vexation on Lamb's face. They took their leave as gracefully as they could, and walked together down the drive.

The two men's annoyance—surely more than the circumstances justified—decided Dawlish to follow them. When they reached the gate, he was only twenty feet away from them. The trees here, were fairly thin, and had they turned they would have seen him. Graham's voice came fairly clearly:

'That young oaf wants a sharp lesson.'

'I thought all along it wasn't the wisest move to butt in. Did you recognise Dawlish?'

'Only as another boorish young man,' said Graham.

Lamb laughed. 'That's where you're wrong. In his way he's quite a celebrity. *The* Patrick Dawlish, in fact. Secret Intelligence and all that. I heard that he was down here, but I didn't think he'd turn up at The Pines. There's more trouble there than they've admitted.'

'Could be,' said Graham, perfunctorily. 'I must admit that I was wrong to go—and I shall not go there again. As for the young woman, if you care to waste your time on her that's your affair.' He glanced along the road as Dawlish heard the sound of an approaching car. He saw Graham stiffen, and then the man turned hastily, re-entered the drive, and stepped up the bank. Lamb stared after him, as if astonished. The car came into sight, and slowed down.

It was Bland's Lanchester.

'Excuse me, sir.' Bland's face appeared at the open window. 'Could you be good enough to direct me to a house called The Pines?'

'This is The Pines,' said Lamb.

'Oh, indeed! How fortunate! A thousand thanks.'

'It isn't a very good time to call,' said Lamb. 'There's been a shooting accident, and the doctor and the police are there.'

'I don't wish to see anyone except a visitor—a Major Dawlish,' said Bland. 'It is *most* important that I should see him, most important.'

The strident blast of a car horn sounded, as an ambulance grazed past them. Bland looked after it, worriedly. 'Most important,' he repeated.

'I'm afraid I can't help you,' said Lamb. 'but I know Dawlish was there a few minutes ago.'

'He was? Then I will risk it,' said Bland. 'Thank you, my dear sir, thank you for your courtesy!'

Dawlish turned and hurried back. He was half-way up the drive by the time the Lanchester had started up. He stepped from the bank quickly, immediately in its path. Carr put on the brakes, while Bland thrust his head through the window.

'Major Dawlish! How fortunate, how fortunate!' He opened the door and jumped down, advancing with hands outstretched.

'Drive on to the house,' Bland instructed his chauffeur, 'the Major and I will walk up.'

'My dear Major,' boomed Bland, 'I have a most sincere apology to make, I have indeed. I am of course referring to my over-zealous plea for the house. I should not have made it. My enthusiasm ran away with me! I hope you will forgive and forget!'

'You certainly spoke in no uncertain terms,' Dawlish said mildly.

'Alas, I must admit it,' said Bland. 'I wish I could make you understand how much I regret my words!'

He stood back a pace, with his hands outstretched; and as he stood there, a familiar sound broke the quiet: the sound of a shot!

Bland jumped. 'What—'

The bullet actually touched him on the cheek; blood welled up and began to trickle down. Bland turned startled eyes towards the sound of the shot, as another bullet struck a tree not a foot from his head.

'Get down, you fool!' roared Dawlish.

He flung himself forward, grabbed Bland's legs, and brought him crashing to the ground. Another shot winged over their heads. For a moment they lay there, breathless, and then someone shouted, and Ted Beresford appeared, running fast and brandishing a gun. There was no more shooting. Dawlish got to his feet and followed in Beresford's wake, but as he ran, he felt an astonishment which made it hard for him to concentrate on the immediate task.

Those bullets had been fired at Bland.

They had come from an automatic, at fairly short range, and so close to Bland that it was impossible to think anything else. There was no apparent sense in it, but as Dawlish rushed the bank on the far side of the drive, a few yards behind Beresford, one thing flashed through his mind. Graham had dodged out of Bland's sight, and might still be in the woods. For that matter, Lamb might have come up the drive and fired. Dawlish was desperately anxious to catch a glimpse of the gunman, but suddenly he came up against a high brick wall.

Both Dawlish and Beresford leapt for a bough of an over-hanging tree and looked over. A small meadow lay on the other side, in which a few cows were grazing, but there was no other sign of life. Thickets lay beyond, and it would have been easy enough for the attacker to hide successfully.

Dawlish saw the chimneys of a large house. He had no doubt that the house was Graham's. As he watched, he wondered what had really brought the two men to The Pines; shooting was surely not so unusual in wooded country.

There seemed little use in staying. Dawlish lowered himself at arms' length and dropped to the ground. Beresford followed suit. Soon they were strolling towards the drive. The grounds of The Pines were surprisingly large. It must be years since they were cleared.

'It's a wonder the trees weren't cut down for timber,' Beresford said. 'Most other patches of pines about here have gone. I wonder why they spared The Pines?'

Dawlish shot him an odd, calculating look.

'Now what have I said?' asked Beresford.

'You've started an idea,' said Dawlish. 'Why were these trees spared, indeed? And why was The Pines taken over by the authorities in the first place?'

'A lot of large, empty houses were,' said Beresford, prac-tically.

'But why were they so anxious to keep this place hidden?' persisted Dawlish. 'I think we can pull a little weight at the War

Office and find out more about the use they put The Pines to,' he went on. 'I—hallo, what's that?'

They reached a small clearing. Trees had been cut down for several square yards, and in the middle was a round hole with a heavy concrete lid, sunk just below the level of the ground.

'Ho-ho!' said Beresford. 'Secret tunnels.'

'Or a disused well,' said Dawlish. He pulled at the cover, but could not move it.

'Lend me a hand, will you?'

Beresford got one side, Dawlish the other, and together they were able to lift the lid. It was about three feet in diameter and several inches thick. Dawlish went down on his knees and examined the hole closely.

'It's not a well,' he said. 'It's cemented round, and that's been done fairly recently. Have you got a torch with you?'

Beresford handed over a pencil torch, and Dawlish aimed a thin beam of light downwards. The light failed before the bottom was sighted, and he picked up a small knob of wood and dropped it; the sound, as it landed, came fairly soon. 'So it isn't very deep,' said Dawlish. 'I find this rather interesting. We'll most certainly have another look later.' He lengthened his stride, adding: 'How did you manage with the prisoner?'

'We were lucky enough to find a disused gamekeeper's hut in the grounds, and locked him in.'

'We'll see the gentleman as soon as we can,' said Dawlish. 'You'd better make sure he can't escape, and then bring Tim back to the house. We don't want the police to get an idea that we're playing tricks with 'em.' He chuckled. 'What happened in London to bring young Keen down here?'

Beresford's story took little time to tell.

He and Jeremy had gone to watch Barry Keen's flat, hoping to follow him to some rendezvous where they could pick up an acquaintance with him. It was quickly evident that he was in trouble. He had left the block of flats in almost a run, his expression terrified. He had been followed. One of his pursuers had caught up with him, and after a heated argument, induced him to return. A loud voiced altercation had ensued. Then the four of them had come out.

Suddenly, and without warning, Barry Keen had jumped on to a passing taxi. The move had taken his companions by surprise. They had followed, however, and caught him up at Waterloo, boarding the same train. At Godalming Keen had out-manoeuvred them, slipping from the train to a taxi. They had secured another, Ted and Tim a third. Realising he was still being followed, Keen had left the cab and dived into the woods, a few hundred yards from The Pines.

'From then on, we all seemed to dog each other,' said Beresford. 'There was no sign of shooting until we got here, but I'd seen that all three of the tough guys were carrying cases.'

'Hmm, well, lucky there weren't tommy guns in them. Now you'd better nip off for Tim before you're spotted.'

Dawlish reached the house to find two policemen standing in the porch, and a third hovering round the windows. In the drawing-room, with one prisoner, was a slim, alert-looking man who introduced himself as Inspector Hall.

He smiled pleasantly at Dawlish.

'Did your friends have any luck with the fellow who got away?'

'I'm afraid not,' said Dawlish, sorrowfully.

'That's a pity,' said Hall, 'but I suppose we shouldn't grumble, as we've still two of the beggars. The injured one went off in the ambulance with Mr. Keen,' he added. 'I'd be glad to have a statement as soon as you can manage it, Major Dawlish. I believe Superintendent Trivett is coming down from Scotland Yard, and I've had a request not to worry you too much.'

'Too kind,' murmured Dawlish. He launched into an account of what had happened, including Beresford's story, but omitting the attack on Bland, while a sergeant took notes. Three men were to be left on duty in the grounds; there was no need to worry. Hall added that there was a gentleman waiting to see him in the sitting-room.

'Who is it?' asked Dawlish.

He thought it might be Bland, but the Lanchester was not outside.

'Mr. Perry Lamb—who lives nearby,' said Hall. 'Is there anything else you would like me to do, Major Dawlish?'

'Not now, thanks,' said Dawlish. 'You've been more than helpful!' He shook hands, and then walked towards the morning-room. Lamb was the last person whom he expected to find here, and he wondered why the man had not gone home.

Hall stopped outside the door with him.

'Oh, how long did the military stay in this place?' Dawlish asked, absently.

He sensed the change in Hall's manner at once; it was hardly perceptible, but he felt sure that there was a stiffening in his attitude, and that his smile flicked on a little too brightly.

'Oh, only for a week or two,' he said. 'They found they didn't need it, after all.'

CHAPTER ELEVEN

A REQUEST FROM MR. LAMB

Dawlish walked thoughtfully into the morning-room.

When he had first seen Lamb, he had appeared to be a rather light-hearted, feckless, good-natured individual; now there was a seriousness and a purpose about him that had not been there before.

'I'm sorry to worry you just now, Major Dawlish, but I felt that I had to have a word with you.'

'About the shindy here?' asked Dawlish.

'Not altogether,' said Lamb. He hesitated, as if in doubt as to the best way of introducing the subject. Dawlish waited patiently. 'Look here, Dawlish,' Lamb went on at last, 'can I speak in absolute confidence?'

'Provided there's no legal complication,' said Dawlish.

'I think I can reassure you about that. The matter concerns the Harcourts and Sir Raymond Graham.'

'Do go on.'

'Before Harcourt came to live at The Pines,' said Lamb, 'Graham wanted to buy it. He would have demolished the house, and put up something rather different and better. It was a disappointment when he found he could not do this, as he had quite expected it to be on the market after the last owner died.'

'You mean Harcourt's uncle,' said Dawlish.

'Yes. No one who knew the old fellow thought he had any relatives,' continued Lamb. 'It was a surprise to all of us when Simon Harcourt inherited. Well—er—the point is this: I was in with Graham in the matter of buying the land. Our two houses are of rather better quality, you know, and this place is badly neglected, and rather spoils the scene. It *is* rather a blot, isn't it?'

'Some people would think so,' said Dawlish.

'The thing is this, Dawlish—we've heard rumours about the house being sold. We don't want it to get into the hands of jerry-builders, and we wondered if'—he hesitated, and then went on with a rush—'if, as a friend of Harcourt's, you'd put in a word for us. We'll see, of course, that Harcourt doesn't lose on the deal. As you may have noticed, he isn't very friendly towards us. As a matter of fact we were coming up to see him about it this morning when we heard the rumpus. Naturally, when we found what the situation was, we didn't press the matter, but we would be most grateful if you could help us. Do you know whether Harcourt *is* planning to sell?'

'Certainly not yet,' said Dawlish.

Lamb breathed more easily.

'Well, that's a relief. And you will help us?'

'I'm helping Harcourt,' said Dawlish, 'but I don't think I have any great influence with him. Still, some opportunity might crop up. I think you can be sure that if the house does go on to the market, you will have an opportunity of bidding for it.'

'That's *exactly* what I want,' said Lamb, eagerly. 'I'm most grateful to you for passing it on.'

'Oh, that's all right,' said Dawlish.

He watched Lamb walking down the drive, noticing the

jaunty air, as if he had succeeded in his main purpose. Yet the prospects of getting The Pines was no nearer than it had been.

Felicity joined him, on her way from the garden.

'Who on earth was that?' she asked.

Dawlish put his arm about her waist.

'Mr. Perry Lamb, disliked by Simon and fond of Linda. He has just told me a rather too convincing story. Very earnest, very plausible, but I think his real reason for coming was to assure me that he and Graham weren't really attracted by the shooting. I wonder if Graham *did* want to buy The Pines.'

'Oh, yes, he did,' said Felicity. 'Most of our chat over lunch was about Lamb and Graham. Simon doesn't like either of them, and I gathered from Linda that it was because they tried to stop him living here. It wasn't until today that they realised that there might be a connection between this effort of Bland's and the earlier one of Graham's, with Lamb as his yes-man.'

'Yes-man,' murmured Dawlish. 'The first I saw of him tallied well enough with that description, but he didn't behave like a yes-man just now. That affair appears to be quite baffling. Did you know that someone tried to murder our Algernon?'

Felicity stared, wide-eyed.

'A bullet,' drawled Dawlish, 'actually touched his cheek.'

'But who—'

'Graham could have tried it—or Lamb. How do the others feel about him?'

Felicity laughed.

'Linda doesn't dislike him, and Simon thinks he is poisonous, but they aren't very serious about the gentleman. You know, Pat, it's pitiful the way those two love each other, and won't admit it in words.' She pulled him towards the door. 'Come on, darling, your lunch will be spoiled.'

He was half-way through an excellent ragout when Ted and Tim arrived. They recounted over again the story of Barry Keen.

'Will the police make a charge against him?' Linda asked.

'I don't know,' said Dawlish. 'I don't even know what he's supposed to have done. Apparently Bland—or those who work for Bland—can incriminate him, but the police don't know anything against him.'

Linda said: 'Can you—' she broke off, and bit her lip.

'Can I influence Bland?' murmured Dawlish. 'I don't know, but I can try. I shouldn't worry too much,' he added, 'whatever Barry has done will prove insignificant compared with the general brew, so there's no great need for anxiety.'

As Dawlish sent Tim and Ted into Haslemere and Hindhead, to find out from the estate agents if Bland had been trying to buy other property in the district, he hoped he was right.

They were back sooner than Dawlish had expected.

'Did you have any luck?'

'It depends what you call luck,' said Tim, sepulchrally. 'Fawned on by hopeful house agents one minute, practically ordered out of their offices by disappointed ones the next—ah! it's a hard life, sleuthing!'

'Did they get any dope?' asked Dawlish, patiently.

'Pat!' exclaimed Beresford solemnly, 'there has, to date, been a feverish interest in Graham's house and in Lamb's. Offers to buy galore, and at ridiculous prices. Interesting?'

'Very,' said Dawlish. He leaned back in a chair thoughtfully. 'This business seems to be deeper than we realised. I think you'd better go up to town and see Whitey. If any man can tell you what the authorities were doing here, he can. I have a distinct impression that the police know, and that they've had instructions to keep it to themselves. I am beginning to wonder,' he added, smiling, 'whether Trivett's interest in The Pines was quite so casual as he made out.'

'If we're going tonight, we'd better get off,' said Tim. 'I think there's a train about six o'clock.'

Harcourt wheeled himself in, and confirmed the time of the train. He also telephoned for a taxi to take them to the station. He seemed contented enough, as if something of the underlying strain was eased. Dawlish was glad to see it, but wondered what had inspired it. It was possible, of course, that he had at last come to some more definite arrangement with Linda.

The evening passed uneventfully. Two delighted old ladies came to inspect the rooms, and went away promising to call again; Dawlish suspected that they found the walk up the steep drive too much for them. Towards dusk, a middle-aged man arrived on the same mission, a retired Colonel who made his departure when he learned that there was no hot and cold running water in the bedrooms.

No one else called that night, but just after ten o'clock Tim telephoned.

'Any luck?' Dawlish asked.

'Well, I certainly saw the old boy, but he just skated over the question. Reading between the lines, I would say that he knows all right, but that it's still on the secret list. I faded out gracefully, of course. Odd show, isn't it?'

'Very odd,' said Dawlish.

As he rejoined the others, he was frowning. Colonel Whitehead, known to his friends and juniors as 'Whitey', was the Chief of their branch of Intelligence. To say the least, his attitude was curious, but it served to convince Dawlish that they had struck deeper things than they knew when they had responded to Harcourt's appeal.

Dawlish strolled down the drive with Felicity, far enough to learn that the two policemen were still on duty. Then, waiting until the household had retired for the night, he crept out of a side door. He walked cautiously away from the house, following the instructions which Ted had given him, as he headed for the shed where the prisoner was still waiting. Unlocking the door, he stepped inside. There was no sound. For a moment he was afraid that the man had contrived to escape; but he was there, huddled in a corner, the narrow beam from the torch shining on terrified eyes.

The others had made a good job of binding and gagging him. Dawlish rested the torch on a battered oil-drum, and leaned forward.

'Speak in whispers. Do you understand?'

The man nodded.

Dawlish unfastened the gag and then released the fellow's wrists. His arms were numb and he could not move them. Dawlish massaged them gently, helping to restore the circulation.

Presently the man began to talk, muttering, spilling out what Dawlish felt quite sure was the truth, as far as he knew it. There was not, however, a great deal that was useful to Dawlish. He did not know Bland by name, and did not appear to recognise a description of him. He operated with several of 'the boys' on various rackets. He swore that he did not know why Barry Keen had been wanted, but he and the others had received instructions to take Keen to a house in Chelsea. The man was not the leader of the gang, and did not know for whom the job was to be done. He did know that Keen was either to be taken to Chelsea, or else killed. The fact that he admitted that without argument or without defending himself convinced Dawlish that he was being frank.

'What address in Chelsea?' Dawlish asked.

'18 Layer Street.'

'18 Layer Street,' repeated Dawlish. 'Who lives there?'

The man shrugged indifferently.

'How should I know?'

'I hope you're telling the truth,' said Dawlish.

He took some sandwiches and a bottle of water out of his pocket and handed them over. The man fell on the food ravenously. Dawlish waited until he had finished, debating with himself the best thing to do with him. He decided to leave him until the morning, and then question him again, before turning him over to the police. The police would lodge a strong protest, but he did not think Trivett would be seriously perturbed.

The only alternative was to let the man go, and follow him. Dawlish decided to tie him up again—though not quite so rigorously—until the morning.

He had left the hut and was wondering whether to telephone Ted and ask him to visit 18 Layer Street that night, when he was suddenly blasted from his feet by a terrific roar. Gazing upward he saw debris flung to the sky, while beneath, a fierce fire raged where once the hut had been.

CHAPTER TWELVE

MR. BLAND SPRINGS A SURPRISE

Dawlish scrambled to his feet, the light wind blowing from behind him, driving the flames towards the trees. There was no sign of the prisoner, who must have been killed instantaneously, before the fire reached him.

A branch flared up, illuminating the whole scene.

Dawlish thought: This is going to be bad.

He did not doubt that the police would be on the scene within a very few minutes, and he started to stamp out the flames which were creeping along the grass and pine needles. He wondered where the nearest water was, and decided that there was not likely to be enough at hand to put this conflagration out; it might be wiser to hurry to the house to telephone for a fire-fighting unit. Then, beyond the flames, he saw the figures of other men. In a shouted exchange, in which their voices were only just audible above the roar of the flames, he learned that one of them had already sent for help.

It was not long before Linda and Felicity appeared on the scene. None of them talked. Silently, doggedly, they fought the flames. Had the wind been higher, there would have been no chance of saving the woods on that side of The Pines, but they succeeded in confining it to a fairly small space before the fire-fighting unit arrived. Dawlish saw the uniformed men, wearing steel helmets, with relief. The snaky hoses were dragged from tree to tree, in a few minutes the ground in the path of the fire was being soaked with water.

There was no further need for amateur help, and together the three of them, Felicity, Linda, and Dawlish, dragged wearily back to the house.

All were shivering, now that they were away from the fire, and Linda lit a log fire in the drawing-room. By then Harcourt had been helped into a chair, and was anxious to know what had happened.

Felicity and Harcourt knew that the prisoner had been hidden in the shed; it was news to Linda. Her expression matched the bleakness of Dawlish's when he had told them briefly of the suddenness of the attack.

'Why should they want to kill him?' she asked, helplessly.

'To prevent him from talking,' said Harcourt.

'But if they knew he was there, why didn't they try before?'

'They probably didn't know he was there until I led the way,' said Dawlish. He glanced at Felicity, who was very pale. Her hair was untidy, and slightly singed, and Dawlish had a sudden, protective urge to pick her up, and carry her away, out of it all. But it was too late for that, they were in it too deep.

Linda suggested that there was no point in them all staying up, and went to help Harcourt to bed again. One of the symptoms of his illness was physical weariness, and he had moved and done much more that day than for a long time.

The sound of the wheeled chair died away.

'Pat,' said Felicity, 'was that bomb aimed at you or at the prisoner?'

'The chances are even,' said Dawlish. 'They may have thought that I was still inside, or it may have been a warning to me.'

Felicity said: 'You don't really think so. If they'd wanted him dead, they would have killed him before you arrived. They certainly wouldn't have let you come out, *after* talking to him, if they just wanted to silence him—there would be no point in it.'

'No,' admitted Dawlish.

'And we aren't even beginning to see the end,' said Felicity.

'You're tired,' said Dawlish, leaning forward. 'Go to bed, my sweet.'

It was at that moment, Felicity rising wearily, that Inspector Hall and Trivett arrived. She passed them with a murmured 'good night', but it was, in fact, past one o'clock in the morning.

Both came forward, friendly and alert.

'Well, now tell me all about it,' said Trivett.

'That's a tall order,' said Dawlish. 'All about what?'

'The fire.' Trivett took out cigarettes, and added casually: 'Had you caught the man who escaped this morning?'

Dawlish nodded.

'And he was in the shed?'

Dawlish nodded again.

Nobody spoke.

'Well,' he said at last, 'no comment?'

'You know you're asking for trouble,' said Trivett.

'I know that, but I thought I might be able to get more out of him than you,' said Dawlish. 'You must believe me when I say that I had no idea that his life would be in danger.'

'No doubt, but I wish you wouldn't take so much in your own hands, Pat,' Trivett said testily. 'It makes it damnably difficult for me. So far, I've managed to get permission for you to carry on, because I think you're as likely as any man to get to the bottom of it, but I can't go too far and this may mean that semi-official support will now be withdrawn. Haven't you got some reason to advance as an excuse for keeping him away from us?'

'None that will satisfy your panjandrums,' said Dawlish.

Trivett shrugged his shoulders.

'You're not being much help. Let's hear the rest of the story, anyway. There might be extenuating circumstances in that.'

Dawlish told him all that he knew, with the exception of the attack on Bland, and the fact that Graham and Lamb had received offers for their houses. By the time it was finished, a clock in the hall struck half-past two. He felt tired and washed-out, and was glad when Trivett called a halt and left with the local inspector. Trivett had good reason to be worried by the official reaction to the death of the man in the shed.

Dawlish had more; in the past, he had worked mostly with official backing; now he was a private individual, and Trivett had made it clear that the affair would be judged from that point of view. If his superiors decided to take a strong line, it might prove more than awkward. Heavy-hearted, Dawlish went upstairs, forgetting that he had intended to telephone Beresford or Jeremy about Layer Street.

He slept so soundly that he was hardly disturbed when Felicity got up in the morning, and it was a little after ten o'clock when she woke him up, with some tea. She was looking very pretty, her hair ruffled at the tips, in a flowered smock borrowed from Linda.

''Morning, darling. Any post?'

'None, but three callers for rooms,' said Felicity. 'I don't think any of them are of any interest to us, though. One is coming back, the others turned it down.'

'Hum. That looks like the end of a bright idea,' said Dawlish. 'By George, I'm hungry!' He drank his tea, had a quick bath and shave, and was downstairs soon after half-past ten. Linda had gone out. Harcourt was in the garden, using a hoe with a short handle. Intent on his task, he looked well and handsome.

Three policemen were still on duty. There was nothing left of the hut, but by the side of the charred ruins, neatly piled together and covered with sacking, were the blackened bones of the prisoner.

Dawlish walked away, more affected than he had expected.

A car was coming up the drive as he reached the house, and he recognised the Owens. He waited for them, greeting them from a distance with a friendly wave. As they drew nearer he saw something akin to excitement on their faces. The car pulled up, and they climbed out quickly, hurrying towards him.

'I say, Dawlish,' said Owen, 'you'll never believe what has happened. It's a most incredible thing.'

'Good or bad?' demanded Dawlish, quickly.

'You be the judge,' said Owen, and took a folded letter from his pocket. 'Have a look at that!'

Thoughtfully, Dawlish ran his eye down the sheet of paper, noticing that both Felicity and Harcourt were watching with unconcealed interest.

Pinned to it was a pink cheque. '*Pay to Maurice Owen, Esq, the sum of Seven Thousand Pounds*' he read. He stared at the signature, bold flourishes in purple ink. '*Algernon L. Bland*'.

'What *is* this?' he demanded, and turned to the letter.

This appeared to be even more startling, for Bland had written:

Dear Mr. Owen,

Since my visit to you yesterday morning, Major Dawlish has performed a great service for me. To express my gratitude to him, I have decided to make him a present of the house which he is so anxious to buy. I am, therefore, enclosing my cheque for £7,000 and trust you will accept this as payment on behalf of Major Dawlish.

A thousand apologies for my rudeness, and a thousand thanks
for your forbearance.

Algernon L. Bland.

'The man must be unbalanced!' exclaimed Owen. 'I say, Dawlish,
do you think it's a hoax?'

'I doubt it,' said Dawlish.

'What did you do for him?' asked Mrs. Owen.

'I knocked him down,' said Dawlish, and added with a grin:
'Someone was shooting at him.' He beckoned to Felicity, while
the Owens stared at him in bewilderment. 'I've never met anyone
quite like Bland,' he admitted, helplessly. 'What do you think, Fel?'

'For once,' said Felicity grimly, 'I am completely at a loss!'

'There is a curious sincerity about the man,' said Dawlish,
slowly. 'He's an odd mixture of crook and philanthropist. His
talk isn't all hot air. If it is mostly fantasy, there is still some
truth.' He handed back the cheque. 'Present it, anyhow, and see
what happens.'

'I'll pay it in on the way back,' said Owen. He seemed to
become aware for the first time of the burnt and blackened trees,
and said abruptly: 'I heard there was trouble here, but didn't
want to put my oar in if it wasn't wanted. Anything I can do?'

'Not really,' said Dawlish warmly, 'though it's jolly decent of
you to offer.'

He wished he could tell them a little more of the situation,
and had they been staying longer at Four Ways, he might have
done so. He had already telephoned to Ted and Tim, about
Layer Street, and was expecting word from them. He was also
expecting further word from Trivett, and until he heard from
the Yard man he felt that it would be wise to act cautiously.
There was one thing, however, that he could do successfully, and
without incurring the wrath of the police: he could visit Graham.

He walked thoughtfully down the drive, after the Owens had gone. There was an unreality about the whole business which harassed him. The cheque from Bland was one of those things which defied understanding; it might well be a gesture on the man's part, because of the shooting incident; yet it might also be an attempt to bribe Dawlish into taking a lesser interest in what was going on. Anything Bland did was likely to have a double motive.

He found Graham's house to be a Georgian building in excellent condition, the gardens surrounding it meticulously and expensively tended.

Graham appeared to be a rich man.

A manservant opened the door, took his card, and went upstairs. Dawlish waited in the wide hall hung with family portraits. Here was wealth, unostentatious but quite apparent.

'Sir Raymond can see you, sir,' said the servant, as he reached the hall again. 'Will you please come with me?'

Following up the curved staircase, Dawlish had an impression of age and spaciousness. This was a good house to live in; that it was out of character with Graham, who had seemed to him supercilious and too conscious of his position, only emphasised the fact that first impressions were notoriously untrustworthy.

Graham was in a book-lined study, sitting at a fine desk of highly polished walnut. A huge fireplace held a few smouldering logs, in spite of the warmth of the day; but the room was north, and it struck cold after the sunlight.

Though his manner was as frigid as before, yet it seemed to Dawlish that he caught a glimpse of something lurking in his eyes, some concealed fear or nervousness.

The greetings over, Dawlish smilingly accepted a chair and a cigarette.

'Thank you. Have you lived here long, Sir Raymond?'

'All my life,' said Graham. 'That is a curious question.'

'I wondered how well you knew Simon Harcourt's uncle,' said Dawlish.

'Not very well. He was something of a recluse, and had little to do with his neighbours,' said Graham. 'I am rather at a loss to understand why you want to know.'

'There's some mystery next door,' said Dawlish, 'and I'd like to help to straighten it out.'

He was wondering how he could best ask what offers Graham had received for his house. It was essential to choose a moment when he was off his guard. The problem was to put him off his guard; he gave Dawlish the impression of being both wary and on edge.

'I know of no mystery,' said Graham. 'It is certainly not an attractive house, but it has an excellent position, and speculative builders would pay large money for it. As I believe Mr. Lamb told you yesterday, I would like to prevent that. I must thank you for your promise to intercede on our behalf, Major Dawlish.'

'I can probably do little,' said Dawlish, 'but—'

The door behind him opened. Graham looked up, as if in surprise, at the sound of a woman's rich, throbbing voice:

'Raymond, darling, I—' She broke off abruptly. 'Oh, I'm so sorry! I had no idea anyone was here.'

'That's all right, Belle,' said Graham.

He seemed a different man, as if the sight of this woman—no longer young, but superbly beautiful—had softened his whole nature. But it was not that which affected Dawlish so much; it was the fact that the woman's Christian name was the same as that of Bland's wife.

CHAPTER THIRTEEN

REPRIMAND

Graham followed the woman from the room, and was gone for ten minutes.

When he returned his eyes and his voice still carried some part of the happiness her presence had brought him.

'Do sit down, Dawlish,' he said. 'I'm sorry we were interrupted.'

'I hope I didn't inconvenience your wife,' said Dawlish.

Graham stared at him for a moment; and the mask dropped back; bleak, lifeless, cold.

He said deliberately: 'I am a widower, Major Dawlish.' That was all. 'Now, what can I do for you? If you only seek information about Julius Harcourt, I am afraid that I can do nothing.'

'Not only that,' said Dawlish. This was the moment to take advantage of Graham's well-covered up discomposure and fire his question: 'How often have you received offers for this house, Sir Raymond?'

He had pierced the screen. Graham clenched his hands. At first Dawlish thought he was going to deny that such an offer had been made, but apparently he thought better of it, for he said:

'Did Lamb tell you about that?'

'No. I thought it possible, and made inquiries.'

'It is no one's business but my own,' said Graham. 'However, you have perhaps some justification in putting the question, and I have no objection to answering. I received two very good offers for my house, one a year ago, one much further back. I believe that the intention was to turn it into a country club or hotel. I refused, of course. Is that what you wanted to know, Major Dawlish?'

'Largely—and I'm very grateful,' said Dawlish. 'I wonder if you remember the name of the man who made the offers?'

'They were separate offers.'

'Made by different men for different interests?'

'I do not know. The first came from the Merrick Estate Company Limited, of which I know nothing. I do not remember the name of the man who made the second attempt. As far as I know, he was not connected with the Company.'

'I see,' said Dawlish. 'It's a pity, because someone is trying to buy The Pines, and I'm anxious to find out whether the same people are interested in your house. Does the name *Bland* call anyone to mind?'

'No one at all,' said Graham.

He was lying; Dawlish had no doubt of that. There was, of course, just the possibility that he knew Bland by a different name, but he did not think it likely.

Graham looked pointedly at a small clock on his desk.

'Is there anything else, Major Dawlish?'

'I don't think so,' said Dawlish. 'Thank you for your help, Sir Raymond.'

Graham pressed a bell, and Dawlish left, intrigued by all that had happened. It was a curious business in every respect.

He reached The Pines and saw a familiar green Morris standing outside. Trivett was there.

*   *   *

Trivett had been back to London and made his report to Scotland Yard. He looked tired, but he was smiling, and Dawlish was surprised at the extent of his own relief.

'All safe?' he asked.

'An official reprimand,' said Trivett, 'but I don't think you need take it too seriously. The truth is, Pat, you've got us all eating out of your hand!'

Dawlish said gently: 'The truth is, William, that the All-Powerful Ones think I might bring the bacon home. If they were sure that you could do without me, they would do more than issue a reprimand.'

'Oh, come!' said Trivett. 'Isn't that a spot conceited?'

'Mock modesty has never recommended itself to me,' said Dawlish, 'nor over much of the other kind, when facts stare one in the face. Who, for instance, is more likely to find out whether Harcourt or Linda Keen are keeping something up their sleeves? You or I? Bland is not a proved rogue—you would have to go very cautiously and carefully in questioning him, but I am in a position to force something from him. All right, Bill, let's forget it—I'm glad that I haven't been formally refused the right of entry into the business!'

Trivett said: 'What makes you think that Harcourt or the girl might be keeping something back?'

Dawlish smiled sweetly.

'Nothing,' he said, 'but it's the kind of notion which might captivate you and Hall.'

Trivett grew suddenly serious.

'Don't overdo anything, Pat,' he warned. 'You haven't got *carte blanche*, you know.'

'I will act with the great circumspection,' Dawlish said lightly. 'Now, out with it, Bill. What's the trouble?'

'My dear chap, how should I know?' demanded Trivett. He laughed with forced heartiness. 'If we knew that, would you—according to your argument—have been let off as easily as you have been?'

Dawlish shrugged his shoulders.

'I suppose if you've had instructions to say nothing about it, I can't ask you to tell me, but it would be handsome of you.'

Trivett looked at him squarely.

'Sorry, Pat.'

'That's confirmation enough,' said Dawlish, breaking into a smile, 'and I won't ask for more. Are you going to work down here all the time, or are you leaving it to Hall?'

'I'm leaving the local business to Hall,' said Trivett.

When Trivett had gone, Dawlish strolled with Felicity through the woods, towards the scene of the fire. Beyond it was another high wall, and beyond that an attractive house ringed by beech trees.

'Lamb's place,' said Dawlish.

'Are you going to see him?'

'Not yet. There's plenty of time for that. If you'll listen a moment, I'll bring you up to date on all the extraordinary things that have been happening.'

Listening with half an ear, Felicity could see that he was pleased at knowing that the crimes were widespread. This was no insignificant undertaking, no isolated instance of misguided private enterprise. It was part of a scheme of some importance, and the police as well as the Intelligence Department knew something about it.

'One thing is firmly established,' Dawlish told her, 'and that is that I would not have been allowed to continue working, after the death of my prisoner, unless they really thought I had a chance of finding out who is behind it. Another thing is reasonably certain. Bland is after something; and others are after him. Hence the shooting.'

'Yes,' said Felicity, rather dubiously. 'Pat, do you think Graham shot Bland because of Bland's wife?'

'Passion motive?' said Dawlish. 'It could be. But I doubt whether it is quite as simple as that. There are other possibilities.' What they were he did not disclose, but went on: 'I ought to go to London tonight, sweet.'

'Why?'

'I'm curious about the place where Keen was to have been taken,' said Dawlish. 'Ted or Tim haven't reported yet, and I'm not sure that I oughtn't to be there myself. I think I'll run up if the car is ready. I don't mind leaving you for the night with the police round and about—Hall's men won't let anyone get into the house.'

'If it weren't for Simon, I would come with you,' said Felicity, 'but I suppose I'd better let you go on your own. Did Trivett say whether he knew anything about Barry Keen?'

'Confound it. I forgot to ask him!'

'That will be a lot of help for Linda,' said Felicity, reproachfully. 'How soon can you find out?'

'I'll give Bill a ring,' said Dawlish.

He telephoned the Haslemere police station; Trivett was still there. He promised to wait for Dawlish, who then telephoned the garage; the Riley was ready. Dawlish set out, wondering a little uneasily whether he was being altogether wise in leaving the house.

Nevertheless, wise or not, he intended to go.

Trivett, questioned, answered obliquely that nothing was known against Barry Keen. He also volunteered the information that the prisoners were members of a small gang which worked racecourses and the East End.

'Assassins for hire,' murmured Dawlish.

'What did *you* learn?'

Dawlish grinned.

'You've been a long time asking me that, haven't you? As a matter of fact,' he added, soberly, 'I got very little more than you did. I gathered, however, that Keen was to be taken to a house in Chelsea; or else murdered.'

That was news to Trivett.

'18 Layer Street,' Dawlish added, 'and I want to look in there tonight, without police interference. Now tell me that I'm not being frank!'

'You could have told me before,' said Trivett, frowning in concentration. 'I've heard of Layer Street, though I can't remember in what connection. What do you intend to do?'

'Pay a visit,' said Dawlish promptly.

'So you said—but what after that?'

'My dear Bill, you don't expect me to think two moves ahead, do you? I don't know. Who and what shall I find? Bland, or his cronies? A common lodging house? Is it an address from which we will learn a lot, or was it given to the thugs in order to mislead us if they were caught and persuaded to talk? The only interesting thing at the moment,' he went on, 'is that Ted and Tim went to have a look at it, and haven't yet reported. What are *you* going to do about it?'

'I shall have men near,' said Trivett. 'That's what you really wanted, wasn't it?'

Dawlish nodded; he was a little worried. Preferring to work on his own, his indirect request to have police within call was an indication that he was not really sure of himself. He set the thought aside impatiently.

Trivett had a sergeant with him. The sergeant drove his superior's car, and Trivett travelled up with Dawlish, after Dawlish had telephoned the reassuring news that there was nothing known against Barry Keen. They talked little on the journey; the one item of information which Dawlish did pass on was the astonishing gift from Bland—and the fact that he had invited him to join the board of the Merrick Company.

Dawlish did not think that Trivett was greatly surprised about the invitation, but he was astonished by the gift.

'Why on earth should he do it?'

'A repaid debt,' said Dawlish, 'or else a little indirect black-mail. As I've said before, everything Bland does is two-sided. Are you sure you don't know more about him than you've told me?'

'Quite sure,' said Trivett.

Dawlish dropped him at the Yard and went along to Brook Street, where he immediately put in a call to The Pines. Felicity answered. There was still no news from Ted or Tim. When Dawlish rang off he was frowning. The continued silence from his friends began to look as if something had gone badly amiss.

He had hardly replaced the receiver before the telephone bell rang. It was Trivett—and Trivett sounded not a little excited.

'Hallo, Pat!' he said. 'I've found out why Layer Street was so familiar.'

'Ah,' said Dawlish.

'It is a small street with only three large houses,' said Trivett, 'and one of them is the town house of no other than Sir Raymond Graham! There was a burglary there a few months ago. Nothing serious, but the safe was rifled and the contents removed.'

'Well, well!' said Dawlish. 'So Graham comes on the scene.'

He replaced the receiver slowly. The information had height-ened, rather than lessened, his despondency. The lack of news from Tim and Ted was now even more inexplicable; but that was not all. Would Graham, or anyone in Graham's confidence, allow men like the murdered prisoner to know the address? If so, Graham was very sure of himself, and played a much larger part in the affair than had so far been suspected.

Dawlish left the flat abruptly and drove to 18 Layer Street, parking the car a block away.

As he neared the house, he saw that a light was shining from an upstairs room and there were dim glows from other windows.

He walked round the corner, finding that a small service alley ran along the back of the house, which was the middle of the three. He hoped, even at that last moment, to see some sign of his friends. He saw no one. The place was quiet, only the distant hum of traffic was there to remind him how near he was to the busy heart of London. If the police were within call, they were acting with admirable discretion.

'Now I'm here,' muttered Dawlish, suddenly annoyed with himself, 'I don't know what to do!'

Deciding quickly, he opened the gate and walked up to the front door. As his finger left the bell the door opened. A maid stood against the bright light of the hall.

'Good evening,' said Dawlish. 'Is Sir Raymond Graham in?'

'Sir Raymond is out of town, sir. Miss Marion is in.'

'I wonder if she will spare me a few minutes?'

'I will see, sir. Please step inside.'

Dawlish had a curious impression that he had been in the house before. He realised that it was because there was a great similarity in the lay-out, the position of the stairs, the rugs and the furniture, between this place and the house next door to The Pines. It was the same, in a smaller way. There was even a similarity about the portraits which hung on the walls. Again he had an impression of a house that was good to live in.

A girl came from a room opposite the stairs. Charming, well-bred, she appeared to possess all the confidence and poise that was so marked in Graham. There was no doubt of the family likeness.

'Good evening, Major Dawlish. How can I help you?'

'I'm not quite sure,' said Dawlish, with the smile which, when he exerted himself, did so much to win confidence. 'I am on a mission of inquiry, and it's led me here.'

Marion Graham's eyebrows rose a fraction of an inch.

'How strange. But please come in.' She led the way into a small drawing-room, motioning him to a chair. She was genuinely puzzled, and Dawlish was quite sure that she had never heard of him before. He wondered how he could best approach the subject, and decided to be blunt.

'Have you had other mysterious callers today, Miss Graham?'

'As a matter of fact, I have,' she said.

'A large man, and a tall, thin one?'

She smiled. 'Yes. How—'

'They are friends of mine,' said Dawlish, 'whom I expected to get in touch with me. May I ask what time they were here?'

'About noon,' said Marion. 'Major Dawlish, I must really ask for an explanation. Why should you and your friends be interested in this house—or in me?'

Dawlish said: 'The address was given to us in connection with—'

He stopped abruptly, his eye caught by a photograph on a low table. The girl turned her head to see what he was staring at, and her frown deepened.

'Why are you looking like that?' she demanded.

Dawlish stood up slowly and took the photograph in his hands. Even if he had not seen Barry Keen, he would have known that this was Linda's brother.

'Major Dawlish!'

'I'm sorry,' said Dawlish, 'but this has startled me. Do you know this man?'

'There is every reason why I should know him,' said Marion, coldly. 'He is my fiancé.'

CHAPTER FOURTEEN

MARION GRAHAM CONFIDES

It was a delicate moment.

Dawlish could see that the girl was agitated by the fact that he recognised Keen. She appeared, too, to be filled with an anxiety which she had obviously been keeping to herself for some time. A false move now might defeat Dawlish's purpose. He looked at her without smiling, wondering how best to turn the discovery to his advantage.

He said: 'Did you know that he was hurt?'

'Hurt!' she cried, and her eyes were suddenly blazing with alarm. 'Badly? Major Dawlish, please—'

'He was shot, but he will pull through,' said Dawlish.

'*Shot?* How did it happen?'

'He appears to have made enemies,' said Dawlish. 'There's no need to worry about him, I assure you. He is having the best possible attention, in hospital, and is well-protected.'

'Protected,' she said. The word was like a sigh. 'Yes, he needed protection. He was so frightened.' Her hands moved agitatedly. 'When did it happen?'

'This morning.'

She looked surprised.

'When did you last see him?' Dawlish continued, after a pause.

She hesitated, and then her words came swiftly, almost fiercely. All the pent-up emotions of weeks, perhaps months, began to break loose.

'He was frightened of something. I don't know what, he would never tell me, only that he had done something which would lead to trouble. He talked of not being good enough for me, of breaking the engagement. I refused to let him, of course. We went to a theatre—in the middle of April, a Friday evening. We were to have met the next day for luncheon, but he did not keep the appointment. That is the last I have heard of him. Except—' She broke off.

'Yes,' encouraged Dawlish.

'Except for these,' she said.

She picked up a handbag, opened it, and took out three envelopes. She handed them to Dawlish, who opened them, one after the other. All were typewritten notes similarly worded, saying that if she tried to find Keen, it would work to his disadvantage.

'When did these come?'

'One arrived on the Monday after the broken appointment,' she said. 'The second about three weeks ago, the other only yesterday morning.'

'Had you looked for Barry?'

'No. I—I was afraid to do so,' she said. 'I thought it might make it worse for him.'

'So he told you he was in danger.'

'Yes.' She drew in her breath sharply. 'There was so little I could do. My father disapproved of the engagement and I could not turn to him for help. There was no one else in whom I could confide.' She was still speaking rapidly, but now Dawlish got the impression that she was wondering whether she had been wise to talk so freely. 'Major Dawlish. I must ask you—'

'Your father will learn nothing from me,' Dawlish said, gently. 'Don't worry about that. Did your fiancé give you any explanation as to why he was so frightened?'

'No more than I have told you.'

'You've discovered nothing since he disappeared?'

'Nothing,' she said. 'It has been unbearable! Major Dawlish, you're quite sure that he is not seriously injured?'

'Quite sure,' said Dawlish. 'Do you know his sister?'

She stared at him.

'I didn't know he had one. I always understood he had no relatives.'

'Oh,' said Dawlish, surprised. 'Well—do you know a man named Bland?'

'No,' she said.

'Then do you recognise a man who looks like this?' asked Dawlish, and gave another vivid word-picture of Algernon L. Bland.

There was no light of recognition in Marion's eyes, and when he had finished, she shook her head. By then Dawlish was beginning to feel the sense of frustration which had not been far away from him since the beginning of this affair. It was easy to understand that Marion had been afraid to confide in her father, knowing that his disapproval of Barry would take a sharp turn for the worse if he suspected that he was wanted by the police.

He said abruptly: 'What has your father got against him, Miss Graham?'

She did not: reply at once, and Dawlish sensed that she was already repenting her outburst.

'Major Dawlish, are you a policeman?'

'No.'

'Then why are you so interested?'

Dawlish said: 'That's simpler to explain than you might think. I've mentioned Barry's sister, Linda. She lives next door to your Hindhead home.' He ignored the look of astonishment on her face, and went on: 'She, and her cousin Simon Harcourt, have met with trouble of some kind, and asked me to help them. My inquiries led me here.'

'What trouble?' she demanded.

'Simply that someone is going to great lengths to get them out of the house,' said Dawlish. 'Perhaps I should explain that Harcourt is seriously incapacitated from war injuries, and Linda looks after him. Knowing that Barry was in some fear of the police, Linda decided not to approach them, and so called on me. There's one thing I can tell you for certain,' he added. 'The police know of nothing against Barry.'

'It is so bewildering,' said Marion. 'I—I can hardly believe that Barry's sister lives next door to The Grange.' She hesitated, and then went on abruptly: 'Does my father know her?'

'Slightly,' said Dawlish.

'Are they alike?'

'Very much so.'

'He has never said anything to me,' she said.

There was pain in her voice and in her eyes. Dawlish wondered whether he should try to find out more of the relationship between father and daughter, and decided against it. She would probably close up if she thought he were prying too deeply. As it was, they sat in silence for some minutes, and then she surprised him by asking:

'Do you know my father?'

'We met yesterday for the first time,' said Dawlish.

'Does he know that Barry's been hurt?'

'I doubt if he knew who was hurt, but he is aware that there has been trouble,' said Dawlish.

'I see.' She looked at him squarely. 'What do you think will happen? Will Barry be in further trouble when—when he recovers?'

'I hope that he will still be in hospital when the whole business is over,' said Dawlish. 'I don't want it to last long, I've too much to do! Did you know that offers have been made to buy The Grange?'

'Oh, yes,' she said. 'That was before—'

Again she broke off, and again Dawlish could see that she was wondering how much she should tell him.

'Before what?' he prompted, gently.

She said: 'Before the estrangement between my father and me.' The words came stiltedly, but it was clear that she had come to a decision. 'I have an impression that my father is also frightened. Do you think that?'

'It wouldn't surprise me,' said Dawlish.

'My whole world has gone upside down in the last six months!' exclaimed Marion. 'I can't understand it. I—we—we quarrelled first over Barry. Until then we had been really good friends.' She brushed her hand over her forehead. 'It's so hard to believe, even now, that we aren't,' she said. 'Something happened to him, some influence entered his life which I don't know about.'

'Influence?' murmured Dawlish, and then asked quickly: 'Before I forget, do you know a woman whose Christian name is Belle?'

'What made you ask that?'

'The wife of the man named Bland is called Belle,' said Dawlish, 'and I thought—'

'You mean that you met Belle at The Grange,' she said, sharply. 'As I have been so embarrassingly frank, the least you can do is to respond in the same way, Major Dawlish. My father is engaged to be married.'

She said so much more than the actual words: just as Graham disapproved of Barry Keen, so she disapproved of Belle. It showed in her eyes and her manner. He could understand the way the break had come, each reasoning with the other to no avail until now they were like strangers.

'I see,' said Dawlish, gently. 'I'm sorry if I seem to be showing too much interest, Miss Graham, but has he known his fiancée long?'

'About four months, I think.'

'I see,' said Dawlish again. 'The last few months seem crucial indeed.' He stood up, slowly. He was at a loss, not knowing what to say to comfort her, yet knowing how grievously she was hurt. He wished that Felicity were here, for where he felt clumsy and oafish, she would have found a way of helping. He said quietly: 'I assure you again that there is no need to worry about Barry, Miss Graham, and I will find out how quickly you can see him. As for the rest of the unhappy business, it has gone deeper than I realised. I had no idea when I came that I would be touching on subjects so painful to you. I hope you'll forgive me.'

She said: 'It has been a relief to talk.' For the first time, he saw her smile; a youthful smile, fresh and charming. 'I hope you find your friends, Major Dawlish.'

'So do I,' said Dawlish. 'It's an odd business.'

It was more than odd, he thought; something must have gone badly wrong or he would have heard before now from Tim or Ted. It was just possible that they had seen someone and followed them; it was equally possible that they had been lured away to a place from which they could not get in touch with him.

'Can *I* help?' Marion asked.

'I don't see that you can,' said Dawlish, and then he remembered what Trivett had told him about the house. 'Oh, there is one thing—was there a burglary here a few weeks ago?'

'A few months,' she said. 'Father and I were at Hindhead. Nothing of value was stolen, though the burglary worried my father a great deal. He—' she hesitated, and then went on with heightened colour—'He actually accused *Barry* of the theft!'

'Why should he do that?' asked Dawlish.

'I think it was just because he disliked him,' said Marion. After a moment's pause, she added unexpectedly: 'It is nearly eight o'clock. Will you stay to dinner?'

'I ought to go,' said Dawlish.

Yet it was a temptation to stay. She might, either directly or indirectly, tell him more during dinner. He thought, too, that she was lonely, glad to talk to someone with whom it was no longer necessary to keep up pretence.

'Do stay,' she said. 'I—'

There was a tap at the door and the maid appeared, carrying a card.

Marion looked at it, and held it out.

The card was familiar. Dawlish needed only a glance to realise that Algernon L. Bland had either discovered that he was here, or else had business with Marion Graham.

'Shall I see him?' Marion asked.

'I think so, but don't let him know I'm here.'

'I—'

'I'll get behind the screen,' said Dawlish. 'This visit might have great importance.'

CHAPTER FIFTEEN

MR. BLAND BIDS AGAIN

Dawlish moved quickly behind the screen, five seconds before Bland came into the room. He could see well enough through the interstices of the carving, nor did the screen hamper in any way the impact of that booming voice.

Bland, Dawlish learnt, was delighted to make Miss Graham's acquaintance. It was a pleasure which had been long deferred, but none the less appreciated because of that. It was extremely kind of Miss Graham to see him, and he did hope that he was not calling at an inconvenient time.

'And now, my dear young lady,' said Bland, 'let me lose no time in coming to the main purport of my visit. It is an impertinence, in some ways—only my conviction that you are a most charming, a most understanding young lady allowed me to presume.'

'Indeed,' said Marion, coolly.

'I come on a matter of some delicacy, one which concerns you, one which *deeply* concerns you, and also concerns your father. I think one might say, with certainty, that the effect on him is the greater. Miss Graham, I *implore* you to answer my question frankly. I am a man of the world. I am a man of business. I have a deep appreciation of the services which people like your father have rendered to the nation. It saddens me—it *grieves* me—to learn that such gallant soldiers, such wise counsellors, find themselves in difficulties. Miss Graham, how much *money* does your father require to put his affairs in order?'

Marion gasped. Even Dawlish was so surprised that he nearly gave himself away by an involuntary movement. That Bland should have the cool nerve to ask such a question astonished him, although he knew the man's effrontery was almost unlimited.

'You are surprised, perhaps, that I know your father is in difficulties,' Bland went on. 'I have ways and means, my dear young lady, and of course I shall treat the matter in strict confidence. You need have no fear that—'

He broke off abruptly.

'Are you—are you *unwell*, Miss Graham? Do not tell me that you were *unaware* of the difficulties which—'

'I am quite unaware of non-existent difficulties,' said Marion, coldly.

Bland leaned forward with a manner of avuncular concern.

'Miss Graham, I assure you that your father is greatly troubled. It is possible that he has not confided in you, but I beg you not to make the mistake of thinking that I am misinformed.'

Marion said stiffly: 'If you have any business to discuss with my father, I suggest you make an appointment with him.'

'But Miss Graham!' Bland sounded distressed. 'You know your own father. You know the pride which sustains him. You know that to approach him personally would be unwise, if not utterly disastrous. And so, my dear, I come to you, even though

I fully understand what a shock my information must be. My justification being that I am quite sure that you would wish to do everything in your power to assist your father, to help him through a period of great difficulty. Is that not so?'

Marion said nothing, and after a slight pause Bland continued as smoothly as if she had spoken.

'I was convinced of it. Both filial duty and the love you have for your father would ensure that. So, Miss Graham, we have reached some kind of understanding. I know that your father needs financial help, you wish to find out how to help him. I have a proposition to put forward. May I proceed?'

Bland's voice took on a plummy note, as if he realised that he had got over the worst hurdle safely.

'Excellent! And please do believe me when I say that I have only your father's future at heart. I am not discussing this from a *personal* point of view only. I am prepared to pay, you see, much more money than your father's Hindhead house is worth, in order to help him. It is true my wife has fallen in love with it. There, she said, is the house of my dreams!'

Dawlish had difficulty in restraining a snort.

'There and then I was determined to buy it,' said Bland, 'and I wish you to be assured, Miss Graham, that if I wish to buy a thing for my dear wife, then I do so if it is humanly possible. How much do you think your father would accept for The Grange?'

'He has no intention of selling it,' said Marion.

'My dear young lady! You are grievously mistaken. In fact I have been told that he is actually negotiating for its sale now! My fear is that he will sell it at a lower price than it is worth, and so fail in his chief purpose—that of establishing himself in financial security for the rest of his life.'

'I am quite sure you are wrong,' said Marion.

'Your words distress me, Miss Graham, distress me unutterably, because you are mistaken, you know, badly mistaken. Let me say this. I have good reason to believe that your father is in *serious* difficulties—difficulties which might, if they were made public, result in his disgrace. The only way of preventing it is to make sure that he has enough money. Miss Graham, I *beg* you—' He paused dramatically. 'I *beg* you,' he repeated, 'to give your whole attention to the task of saving him from serious trouble. Perhaps he is reluctant, even now, to sell The Grange, because he feels that he holds it in trust for you, his only child. You would not demand such a sacrifice if you knew the stakes. Miss Graham, will you help him by finding out what price he has put on The Grange? Will you do your best to defer any sale, so that I may have an opportunity of considering that price, and by how much I can exceed it? Please, my dear.' Dawlish saw him move forward, with his hands outstretched. 'Will you give me your assurance, your solemn assurance, realising what *might* happen if you refuse?'

The same tactics, thought Dawlish, as he had used before. A show of generosity, and then, like the flicking of a whip, the threat, well wrapped up, but clear enough for Dawlish to see.

'*Will* you?' repeated Bland.

'I—' began Marion.

'*Please!*' said Bland, in a voice which quivered.

What would have followed had there not been an interruption, Dawlish did not know.

There was a tap at the door, followed by the prim, unemotional voice of the maid.

'Miss Lennox has called, Miss Marion.'

Dawlish had a queer impression that she had thrown a bombshell into the room. The impression was created by a faint intake of breath, a sound which was hardly audible, and then a tense silence.

It was Bland who broke it.

'Miss Graham, I think perhaps it would be gracious of me to give you a little time in which to decide. May I have the pleasure of calling on you tomorrow morning, at, shall we say, eleven o'clock? *Thank* you, my dear. Thank you again. Good night! A thousand thanks for your kind attention!'

He walked out, with an air. At the same time Dawlish heard Marion's voice sharp and clear.

'Ask Miss Lennox to wait, Maude.'

Dawlish stood up, glad to stretch his legs. He looked over the top of the screen with an engaging smile, but that faded when he saw Marion's set face.

'A bouncing gentleman,' said Dawlish.

'Yes,' said Marion. 'Yes. If there is any truth in what he says, it is her fault.'

He thought that she had forgotten him; certainly she was in the throes of an inward struggle. The way she said 'her' held more than dislike, and he did not doubt that the word referred to Miss Lennox. He did not seriously doubt, either, that she was the 'Belle' of The Grange.

Abruptly, Marion said: 'Will you stay, please? I do not wish to see her alone.'

'If I can help—'

'Thank you.' Marion stepped to the fireplace and pressed the bell. When the maid appeared, she said: 'Ask Miss Lennox to come in, please.'

Dawlish noted grimly that it was Graham's 'Belle' all right, clad in a mink coat which was worth a small fortune; her hair, her whole appearance, the result of expert and expensive attention.

'My dear Marion,' she said, in her throbbing voice, 'I was afraid that—why, *Major*—' She broke off.

'Good evening,' murmured Dawlish.

'I—I had no idea that you two knew each other.'

'Major Dawlish is dining with me,' said Marion, frigidly.

There was a moment's pause. It was obvious that Belle wished to speak to Marion alone, but finding that now to be impossible, she was prepared to accept—and ignore—Dawlish's presence, rather than give the whole project up. She began rather cleverly, Dawlish thought, her throbbing voice showing just the right amount of hesitation.

'It is a little difficult to plunge crudely into what I came to say, Marion, but, dear child, do credit me with some sincerity in an appeal to relax your hostility towards me. I want you to believe the truth—that I have your father's interests at heart, that I have a very deep and sincere devotion to him. It *is* true, you know. He is distressed because we are always at loggerheads, and I am equally distressed.' When Marion did not answer, she went on: 'My dear, are you being fair to him or to yourself? I do not expect you to change your attitude for my sake, but for his and your own. The whole of your future will be affected if you remain so aloof, so bitterly hostile.'

Marion said tonelessly: 'One cannot switch sides at the drop of a hat. Feeling goes deeper than that.'

The older woman half-turned; Dawlish thought that he read real regret, real sorrow, in her expression.

'I am more than sorry,' she said, 'that you see it that way.'

She wrapped her coat about her, nodded to Dawlish, and walked with a certain regality from the room. The maid opened the front door.

Dawlish turned to look at Marion.

He had rarely spent an hour of such embarrassment; half the

time he had been in this room he had wished himself elsewhere; yet now, as he looked at Marion's ashen face, he felt glad to be here. She was suffering too great a strain to be able to bear it on her own. Stranger he might be; but there was some spark of affinity between them.

Tears were glistening in her eyes.

'Shall I come back later?' he murmured.

'No, please stay.' She moved to the fireplace again and pressed the bell. When the door opened, she said: 'I am ready for dinner, Maude.'

Dawlish smiled, and tucked her arm under his.

'Dinner will do you a world of good,' he said.

It takes a great deal to spoil the appetite of the young. Marion ate with increasing enjoyment, and half-way through the meal she looked at him with a smile so frank and genuinely amused that he was astonished.

'I don't know whether it's dinner or you who's done me good, but *something* has.'

'I would like to think it was I who was responsible, but very much suspect it was the dinner,' said Dawlish.

She smiled.

'I suppose Bland's visit is connected with the mystery about which you talked?'

'I think everyone who spoke, and everything they spoke about to you tonight, is mixed up in it somehow.'

'You mean, Miss Lennox—'

'Belle Lennox,' said Dawlish, 'whom Bland appeared anxious to avoid.'

He thought she was genuinely surprised by the suggestion that Belle might be playing any part beyond the purely personal matter of her engagement to her father. Her mind was chaotically troubled. She was worried about her fiancé; about her father; about the possibility, which Bland had so cleverly planted in her mind, that her father was in financial difficulty; and about Belle.

It was ten o'clock before he rose to go.

He had not said anything directly about Belle, but had, he hoped, increased the possibility that she would one day give the older woman a chance to prove her sincerity. He had obtained her promise to see Bland in the morning. He hoped to be present. If he were unable to get here, she would telephone him at the earliest opportunity. He convinced her that by so doing she would help to clear the mystery both of her father and of Barry.

It was a curious fact that his preoccupation with Marion had, for the time being, driven the mystery of Ted and Tim into the background. He walked along King's Road, thinking of the girl. Nothing she had said and nothing that had happened had helped him greatly. It was not at all surprising that Bland was bent on buying The Grange; it merely proved, in the light of his struggle for Four Ways and The Pines, that there was some big scheme on foot, but further proof of that was really superfluous. Preoccupied by thought, he walked up the stairs to the flat.

Then he saw a streak of light beneath the door.

He pulled up short, his whole body tensed and watchful. He listened with an ear pressed close to the keyhole, but could hear nothing. In the soft landing light he saw bright scratches on the lock of the door, evidence that someone had tried to pick it— and the light suggested that they had succeeded. He took out his key-case and selected the key gently; he did not want to make the slightest sound.

He turned the key.

The door opened slowly. He could hear nothing. He tiptoed slowly forward, without closing the door behind him—and then he heard the first sound, a chink of glass. Frowning, he stepped towards the lounge, from which a stream of thin light was coming.

'I suppose he *will* turn up,' a man said.

It was the voice of Tim Jeremy.

CHAPTER SIXTEEN

A STORY FROM TIM

A wide, satisfied grin spread over Dawlish's face as he looked through the crack of the door. Ted Beresford was lounging in one chair, Tim in another. The gurgling sound of a receptacle filled with beer came to his ears. Silently he stepped into the room and gently lifted the tankard from Beresford's hand.

'Thanks, old chap.'

A startled gasp followed.

'Of all the bloody silly—'

'Yes, yes,' said Dawlish soothingly, 'but you do owe me something. Bosom-thumping hour after hour in worry over your worthless carcasses is thirsty work.' Now that he could see both of them more clearly Dawlish saw that they looked tired and drawn. 'Anything doing?'

'It's not so much "what's been doing",' said Ted bitterly, 'as "who's been done".'

'Oh boy! What a chase we've had!' murmured Tim.

'Ah,' said Dawlish. 'A chase. So it was Number 18 Layer Street that walked away?'

'Not Layer Street,' said Tim. 'A gentleman who visited it just after we did. Your Mr. Lamb,' he added, accusingly. 'We not only discovered that Graham owned the Layer Street house, but actually met his daughter. Then Lamb came along. We would have split up, one following him and one watching the house, but for the fact that Mr. Lamb was already in the process of being followed.'

'Oh,' said Dawlish, 'go on.'

'That's just what Lammikins did, followed by a trailer, followed by us.'

'Where to?' said Dawlish, when Tim paused.

'Wales,' said Tim laconically, 'Cardiff. Without a case, and only the clothes he was wearing. We caught the train by the skin of our teeth. There wasn't time to telephone The Pines, if we were to find out where Lamb was going.'

'Well,' said Dawlish. 'Did you?'

'That's the rub,' said Tim. 'No. I thought we had him nicely taped, but he gave us the slip when he went into a restaurant. There were two exits, and we didn't know it. We kept his follower in sight, and that young man was badly upset, because he also lost Lamb. When he realised what had happened, he made a bee-line for the station, and came back to London. At least,' added Tim, mournfully, 'we thought he came back to London, but when we got off the train he wasn't there. That's a fact,' he added. 'I spent ten minutes and half a crown buttering up a guard, and was told that a passenger had jumped off the train a few miles outside London, when it slowed down with the signals against it.' Tim put down his tankard with a sigh. 'Sorry, old chap, we really thought we had him.'

'The fact that Lamb dodged you and the other fellow,' said Dawlish slowly, 'shows that he knew that he was followed. Interesting. The other man also knew that you were watching him, and made sure you didn't find out where he went. On the whole, they're smart, aren't they?'

'Yes,' said Ted, dejectedly, 'too smart for us.'

'Not really,' said Dawlish. 'We know now that Lamb went to Cardiff. It shouldn't be hard to find out whether he's known to have any business connections there. It's progress of a sort.'

'Kind words indeed. What have *you* been up to?'

Dawlish gave them a brief résumé of what had happened in Hindhead and at Layer Street. They spent ten minutes talking about it, before Tim yawned again and declared that if he didn't turn in he would fall asleep where he was.

They moved off to bed, Tim and Ted sharing the small spare room. Dawlish was practically asleep, lulled by the rhythmic snoring of his guests, when the front door bell rang.

He sat up. The snoring stopped.

The bell rang again as he was putting on his dressing-gown, and for a third time as he reached the hall. By the spare room door, he could see the peering figures of Ted and Tim. He waved them away, smoothed his hair down, and opened the door.

Belle Lennox stood there. With a swift, almost frightened glance over her shoulder, she pushed past him into the hall.

She was wearing the mink coat, and looked as lovely as she had at Chelsea; but now her poise had gone, and she was frightened. Dawlish put a hand to the door—and then he saw a shadow, half-way down the stairs. He slipped to one side, and whispered:

'Ted—take Miss Lennox inside. Tim, bring a gun.'

Tim appeared at Dawlish's side, and the cold steel of an automatic changed hands.

'Really, Miss Lennox,' Dawlish said, as if she were still there, 'this is too much.' He added in a whisper: 'Tim, get her coat and put it on, then come back.' 'No, please!' he added in a louder voice, 'there is little that I can do, at any time, and at such an hour as *this*.' The shadow near the stairs stayed motionless.

Belle took her cue with commendable speed.

'Major Dawlish, you must—'

'There is no must about it,' said Dawlish, peevishly. As he spoke, Tim joined him. Crouching low, and draped in the coat, he looked much the same height as Belle Lennox. 'Be careful as you go out,' Dawlish added with a whisper. Then, aloud: 'I must ask you to go, Miss Lennox.'

Whoever was watching from the stairs must have taken the emerging figure to be that of a woman. This was the dangerous moment. If murder were intended, the attempt would come now.

None did.

'Go down,' whispered Dawlish.

He switched off the light; only the faint landing light remained. He slipped on to the landing as Tim reached the head of the stairs, keeping close to the wall. Tim, his face hidden, went down the stairs. Dawlish, creeping closer, saw the man who was waiting. It was no one he recognised.

'So that was just a waste of time,' the man said, in a low-pitched voice, 'perhaps you'll do what *I* tell you in future.'

There was a moment's pause; Tim waited, not quite sure what Dawlish wanted him to do. Dawlish said, in his normal voice:

'Take him, Tim.'

In spite of the poor light, he was able to see the astonishment on the face of the man as Tim gripped him firmly above the elbow.

After one furious attempt to get away, he appeared to be submissive enough, however, giving Dawlish the impression that he was both frightened and bewildered. Dawlish watched him coming up the stairs, guided by Tim, with great satisfaction. The satisfaction was increased when Beresford switched on the hall light, and exclaimed:

'Well, well! if it isn't our little man from Cardiff!'

Tim propelled him on into the room where Belle Lennox was standing. Dawlish looked at her quickly. She was not so pale, but her agitation was fairly evident. She looked at the captive, who avoided her eyes; and then she glanced at Dawlish.

'He followed me from my flat,' she said. Her voice lacked its usual vigour.

'Do you know him?'

'Until tonight, I had never seen him.'

'H'm.' Dawlish looked at the man searchingly. There was a curious likeness between him and the unfortunate man who had led the attack on Barry Keen, and, later, been murdered in the hut. It could be coincidence, but that was unlikely.

Ted, still holding the automatic, and Tim with a ferocity the coat had concealed, crowded near their prisoner. Nothing could have been better calculated to inspire fear.

Dawlish said, lightly: 'You must answer, you know. Why did you follow Miss Lennox?'

The man did not reply.

'All right, let's try it this way,' said Dawlish. 'Who ordered you to follow Miss Lennox?'

The man said: 'I—I don't know.'

'Now, come!' said Dawlish, reasonably. 'You don't go about London following lovely ladies at the order of someone whom you don't know. The truth might help you; lies and evasions certainly won't.'

'I tell you I don't know! It—it was my job for tonight. I didn't want to do it, I'd done plenty today already.'

'Yes. Following Perry Lamb,' said Dawlish. 'Why did you come back from Cardiff so quickly?'

'I lost Lamb, and these two fellows were watching me,' he said. 'I had to throw them off.'

'Eminently reasonable so far,' said Dawlish, 'but I want it to go a bit further.' He grinned. 'Let's make a new start. What is your name?'

'Crabb—Tom Crabb.'

'Have you a police record?'

'I—yes.'

'Is it a recent one?'

'I haven't been inside for three years.'

'Hmm, not always irrefutable evidence of good behaviour,' said Dawlish. 'You've been paid to stand by and wait for orders, haven't you? You've done a little gang work, with several others, but you, your brother and at least two friends were on the special staff—kept in reserve for really big jobs. Isn't that right?'

Crabb threw him a startled glance.

'Quite easy,' Dawlish told him. 'I recognised the likeness. He was one of three who followed Barry Keen yesterday, with orders to kill him. Why weren't you there?'

Crabb said: 'I'd been on duty all night—I was resting.'

'That's a lucky thing for you,' said Dawlish. 'Otherwise you would be getting ready for another prison sentence, whereas now you've half a chance of avoiding one. Half a chance, remember. You look a fairly sensible chap,' he added, seriously. 'Surely you don't *like* dodging the police, taking orders from someone whom you don't know, always being on guard—or do you?'

Crabb cried passionately: 'If only I could get away from it all!'

'You can,' said Dawlish, 'if you behave yourself from now on, and if you talk freely.'

'There—there's so little I know!'

Dawlish said, gently: 'I think there is one thing you don't know that I do. When your brother went after Keen—'

Crabb burst out: 'You needn't use him against me, that's

what they've done all the time! I don't want to let him down, but there's got to be an end to all this.' He broke off, staring at Dawlish, whose expression was bleak. 'Why are you looking like that? What—what have I said?'

'Your brother was murdered,' Dawlish said.

Crabb took a step forward, one hand raised, as if to fend off evil tidings, his red-rimmed eyes glassy with fatigue and shock.

'Who—' he croaked, and then stopped.

'He was taken prisoner, in the same way as you,' said Dawlish, 'and put into a hut, where I proposed to question him later. He was killed when a bomb was thrown at the hut. It happened quickly, and it was done by someone for whom he worked, someone who wanted to make sure that he could not talk freely.'

Crabb clenched his hands.

'The devils, the devils! I can tell you this much—*Lamb* is something to do with it! It was Lamb who asked us for a Molotov cocktail; it must have been for that.'

'Who do you mean by "us"?' asked Dawlish.

'There are three others. We met him in a village near Hindhead.'

'I see. Why were you following him?'

'He said he thought he would be followed, and he wanted me to lead the trailer away from him.'

'I see,' said Dawlish again. 'So you know why he went to Cardiff? Or where he went when he got there?'

'I know right enough. He went to talk business with one of the big colliery owners. A man named Justin. I don't know why, but I know that's where he was going.'

'Had Lamb been there before?'

'Sometimes.'

'Has Justin ever been to see him at Hindhead?'

'I don't know, but he's been to Lamb's London flat.'

'We're making progress,' said Dawlish. 'Was it Lamb who sent you to watch Miss Lennox?'

'No,' said Crabb, and there was desperation in his voice, because he was afraid that he would not be believed. 'It wasn't Lamb. Someone telephoned me—I've been telephoned before by the same man, so has Lamb. Lamb works for him, too. I swear it's the truth!'

'I don't disbelieve you,' said Dawlish.

Crabb drew in his breath, and then turned piteous eyes on Belle.

'I wasn't going to hurt her,' he said. 'I was told to kill her if she came to see Dawlish, but I wasn't going to do it.'

Dawlish turned and smiled at Belle.

'Murder was what you feared, wasn't it?'

CHAPTER SEVENTEEN

VISIT TO MR. LAMB

'Yes,' said Belle.

Dawlish was gratified that she did not try to evade the issue. There was a directness about the woman which appealed to him. Now she looked at him fearlessly, and then glanced towards Crabb.

'He is speaking the truth, I think. He certainly had several opportunities to kill me. Can you help him?'

'I will try,' said Dawlish.

He knew that the man had probably been a party to murder, violence, and robbery, but to balance this was the feeling that Crabb had never really been a free agent. He remembered that Barry Keen had been tripped up by some trivial crime, and thereafter the ordering of his life had been taken out of his own hands: perhaps this man had suffered in the same way.

Yet—why had Belle asked that question?

Had it been on humanitarian grounds? Or was there some ulterior motive for her wishing the man to be safe?

'I have several things to tell you,' she said, 'but I don't want Crabb to hear.'

'That's all right,' said Dawlish. 'Ted, take him into the other room.' He waited until the man was led out. The 'other room' was fitted with a window with toughened glass, difficult to break and impossible to open once it was locked; and Ted doubtless had locked it. He also locked the door. Dawlish switched on the electric fire and offered Belle a drink. She refused, leaning forward to warm her hands. That she was one of the loveliest women in London Dawlish had no shred of doubt.

'It hasn't worked out as I expected,' she said.

'How often does anything?' asked Dawlish, with an engaging grin. 'You probably had some curious notion that I prefer to break a man's neck first and question him afterwards.'

She smiled.

'Your reputation is somewhat along those lines.'

'According to Algernon Bland?'

Her smile grew set.

'Partly,' she said.

'Are you his wife?'

'No,' she said, 'but a great many people think I am.'

'I see,' said Dawlish, quietly. 'And you went to Graham, on Bland's instructions—'

'Request,' she corrected. 'He doesn't instruct me.'

'I'm sorry—request.' Dawlish lit a cigarette, while the other two men watched him closely. 'You went to Graham with the idea of trying to make sure that he sold The Grange to Algernon Bland. Did you have any luck?'

'No. At first, I tried. I thought that he would be fairly easy to persuade. He—' she broke off, and there was a curious expression in her fine eyes. 'He did not realise what I was after, of course. He is an astonishingly simple man. I am very deeply in love with him.'

Dawlish said lightly: 'That wasn't hard to guess after I had seen your attempt to win his daughter round.' He glanced at Ted and Tim. 'This is a most curious business. None of the normal things work out as they should do. Crabb isn't the black-hearted villain he ought to be; Bland isn't all rogue—'

Belle exclaimed: 'You think that?'

'Well, yes,' said Dawlish. 'I've been at some pains to point out to others that his morality is a kind of café au lait mixture. Am I right?'

'You are absolutely right!' she said. 'He makes vast amounts of money in ways you would not approve'—Dawlish appreciated the carefulness with which she used her words—'and then he gives it away. He made you a generous present, didn't he?'

'Most certainly,' said Dawlish, 'but whether I shall accept it is a different matter.'

'You'll be a fool if you don't,' she said. 'He thinks you saved his life, and he believes that is worth seven thousand pounds. I agree with him.'

'There is the little matter of where the money came from,' said Dawlish, quietly.

She looked surprised.

'Well, he has many legitimate interests and I don't think anyone could prove that he ever made money dishonestly. I shouldn't let an over-scrupulous conscience interfere with that gift, Major Dawlish.'

She broke off, but Dawlish did not speak.

'If I had been told, six months ago, that I would feel as I do about Raymond, I would have laughed.' She shrugged her shoulders. 'But I haven't come to make an emotional appeal to you, Major Dawlish. I came to tell you *something* of what you already guess. I also came to tell you that I am quite sure that Algernon will let *nothing* stand in his way. He wants The Pines;

he wants The Grange. Lamb's is practically his already—Lamb is, of course, involved in this affair. Did you know that?'

'Not until Crabb told me.'

'So Crabb robbed me of my thunder,' said Belle, with a quick smile. 'Well, there it is! Lamb and Algernon are together in this, and there is, of course, someone else. Who, I do not know. It might be this Justin man. I do know that Algernon is determined to buy that property, as well as several other estates up and down the country. He may give away to charity or to some deserving causes practically all the profit he makes, but he is going to do his utmost to get it. He has paid you seven thousand pounds for saving his life. That cancels out his debt to you, in his opinion. I know that he hopes you will be sensible, as he calls it, and that you will withdraw, after persuading Harcourt to sell. If you don't—' She broke off, with a shrug. 'I hope I needn't cross the t's and dot the i's.'

'You needn't,' Dawlish assured her, 'but I will. You know, don't you, that what you and Crabb have said makes it evident that it was Algernon who tried to murder Barry Keen?'

'Nonsense!' said Belle, roundly.

Dawlish smiled, in no way put out.

'I know that the complications have gone beyond superficial reasoning, but there it is—if we read from the surface. Algernon and Lamb work together. They employ Crabb and his fellows, three of whom set out to murder Barry Keen, and all but succeed. Those things are facts.'

Belle said, slowly: 'Aren't you forgetting the unknown man about whom Crabb talked?'

'If he exists. I think we shall soon find that out. It might be Lamb himself or it might be Algernon Bland, speaking in an assumed voice.'

'That isn't like Algernon,' Belle protested. 'He would hardly use terrorist methods.'

Dawlish grinned.

'It is exactly like him. If he wants a murder done, it would be characteristic of him to give the orders under the guise of an alias. He tries to deceive himself, so he would certainly try to deceive others. You must at least admit that this mysterious unknown *might* be Algernon L. Bland.'

After a pause, Belle said:

'It is, I suppose, a possibility, though in my opinion a remote one.'

'There is the other angle,' said Dawlish. 'Someone tried to kill Bland. Shots came at him from the wall of Graham's house. Graham had the opportunity. So did Lamb, and as I've said before, there might have been others as yet unknown to us. Does Graham know that you know Bland to the extent that you have told me?'

'No!' she said, a little too quickly.

'Does he suspect it?' demanded Dawlish.

'I don't think so,' said Belle, 'and I do not believe that Raymond Graham would attempt murder, or violence of any kind. Certainly not for that motive. He is the type to face it openly.'

'Soul of honour, yes,' murmured Dawlish. 'Sorry, Belle!' he added, when he saw her sudden change of expression. 'That was cheap, but I was speaking off the record. Well—why did you come to see me?'

'I've told you—so that I could let you know as much as possible of Algernon's intentions. If you like, because I thought you ought to understand that nothing is likely to stop him from going on with this. I don't know why he wants this land, only that he wants it so much that he has convinced himself that he must have it. I think,' she added in a soft voice, 'the fact that he asked me to work with Raymond is evidence of that. He hardly expects Raymond to be satisfied with holding my hand.' She hesitated, and her expression saddened. 'You must find this most embarrassing, Major Dawlish, and the truth hard to believe that I did not expect Raymond to fall genuinely in love with me, or that I would do the same with him. I have been quite frank with you.'

'Yes,' Dawlish said. 'Yes, I know, and I warmly appreciate it. Yet you were frightened of Crabb.'

'I was frightened of being followed and killed.'

'Knowing who Crabb was?'

'Yes,' she said, 'knowing that he has worked for Algernon. But I am quite sure that Algernon would not give him instructions to injure me, that is why I am convinced that there is someone else, someone unknown behind it. You see?'

'I see,' said Dawlish, slowly. 'Well—we don't seem to have got much further, but we've made a little progress. Would you care to stay here tonight? We can offer you—'

'I must go to my flat,' she said, 'but I would be grateful for company on the way, Major Dawlish.'

'But of course,' said Dawlish, at once.

He left with Belle a few minutes afterwards. He did not speak to Tim or Ted, but he knew that they were following. Belle's flat was in Park Lane, only ten or fifteen minutes' walk from Brook Street.

The woman said nothing for the first five minutes. Few people were about, and only once or twice did a taxi pass them. Shadowy figures sometimes loomed up in the darkness, but now that she had Dawlish with her, Belle did not seem in any way afraid.

At the entrance to the block of flats she halted.

'So kind of you. I shall be all right now.'

'I'll make a job of it,' said Dawlish. 'They might use more men than Crabb, you know.'

Upstairs, she gave him her key. He explored each room, but as far as he could see, nothing had been disturbed.

'All safe,' he said. 'I think you ought to lock the door and make sure that the windows can't be forced. Anyone else have a key?'

'Only Algernon and myself.'

'And you're quite sure about Algernon,' said Dawlish lightly, 'so there shouldn't be any need to worry!' He smiled and patted her shoulder. 'Don't mind me, I get awkward at times! Tell me, what's Lamb's London address?'

'He has a service flat in Farm Street, St. John's Wood. Number 31.'

'Thanks,' said Dawlish. He half-turned, but looked back when she made an involuntary step forward. 'Yes?' His tone was inviting.

'I don't know how well you know Marion,' she said, quietly, 'but if you can persuade her to think less disapprovingly of me, I would be more than grateful.'

'Right! I'll see what I can do. Did you know she was engaged to Harcourt's cousin?'

She looked astonished.

'I had no idea it was the same Keen. Of course, I should have realised it when you told me that Marion's fiancé had been attacked, but—'

'We can't take everything in at once,' said Dawlish. 'It's a curious fact though, isn't it?'

He made his way thoughtfully down the wide flight of stairs. Ted and Tim were in the dimly-lit hall. They anticipated his request that one of them should stay there overnight, and had already decided that it should be Ted. With Tim, Dawlish walked along Park Lane, towards Marble Arch.

'Whither away?'

'I thought we'd have a look at Lamb's flat.'

Dawlish was preoccupied with the various things that had happened that night. A night of embarrassing confidences, he reflected—less surprising from Belle than from Marion. Belle knew now that she was playing for high stakes. She wanted to put the past behind her, and to marry Graham. She was afraid of what would happen when Bland realised it. Dawlish was by no means certain that she was as confident as she pretended that Bland would do nothing to injure her. If he discovered that she was prepared to throw him over for Graham, he might become vicious solely because of jealousy. He was a man who would expect complete control over any and everything which he considered belonged to him.

Yes; that motive alone would be strong enough to make him want to kill Belle.

There was, Dawlish admitted, the possibility that he would seek revenge more cunningly. He might prefer to do all he could to hurt her, by injuring Graham. Dawlish turned from this thought to the fact that Bland was at all costs determined to buy the houses and the land near Hindhead. First he had employed the method of direct approach and offers to buy, allied to threats when there was stubbornness on the part of the owners. Then, with Graham, he had tried to work through Belle and through his daughter. Dawlish did not think there was any serious doubt that young Keen had been given the task of winning Marion's support. Just as Belle had fallen in love with Graham, so Keen had fallen in love with Marion. There was little doubt that he had refused to do what he was told. Equally, there was little doubt now, in Dawlish's mind, that he had threatened to tell Marion the truth, and that rather than permit it, he had been attacked.

One mystery remained in that connection; why had he to be shot *or* taken to 18 Layer Street?

Dawlish thought there was a simple explanation; that Keen had been given the chance of either seeing Marion again and getting her to influence her father, or, if he refused, of being liquidated. He had not had the moral courage, after all, to tell Marion everything. Rather than be forced to go to Layer Street, under escort, he had made his desperate attempt at escape.

'I wish I knew how he was,' Dawlish said suddenly.

'Who?' asked Tim obligingly.

'Barry Keen. The police will probably learn a lot from him before they tell me the first thing he says. Oh, well,' he added philosophically. 'Look! A taxi!'

He let out a stentorian bellow, and the taxi pulled up. Rejoicing, Dawlish and Tim climbed in, and were driven to Farm Street. It was not difficult to find Number 31, and the driver promised to wait for them. They went into the house, an old one which had been converted into flats; there was a restaurant, still open, in the basement. A small red sign indicated a flight of steps leading to it.

The hall of the house was badly lit. They stood for a moment looking at the name-boards, until they saw 'Perry Lamb' written on the top one; he was on the third floor.

The steps to it were of stone, and it was impossible to conceal their presence. Dawlish did the sensible thing, and walked naturally. None of the flats showed light. They reached the third floor; a single door faced them. Dawlish shone a torch on the key, and frowned.

'Yale lock,' he said, 'and a solid wood door. Not so easy.'

Brushing against it, they saw that it was insufficiently latched. It swung open. Dawlish crept cautiously forward, gun in hand. No one was in the wide hall. He explored further, with Tim in close attendance.

There was no light in any of the rooms, save one. Just a thin, pale glow, and utter stillness. Dawlish advanced cautiously; the whole set-up had all the appearance of a trick, and his visit might have been anticipated.

There was no sound.

He flung the door of the lighted room back, so that if anyone were hiding behind it, it would crash into them, and then strode forward. No one was behind the door, but there was someone in the room.

It was Lamb.

He was sitting at a small table, staring towards them with sightless eyes. His lips were set in an odd smile; there was something ghoulish about that hint of merriment on the face of a dead man.

A knife was protruding from his chest.

CHAPTER EIGHTEEN

QUICK MURDER

Dawlish stood quite still, staring at the body. There was no doubt that Lamb was dead. He turned away and dialled a number.

'Hallo. Is that Paddington Station? Can you tell me when the last train from Cardiff arrived? . . . Yes tonight . . . Eleven thirty-five, thank you.' He replaced the receiver, and glanced at his watch. It was half-past one. 'So he walked right into this,' he said to Tim.

'Are you going to call the Yard?'

'Soon,' said Dawlish. 'I don't like the set-up, Tim, something's wrong about it.'

Together they looked about the room.

Nothing was disturbed.

There was a blank sheet of paper in front of Lamb, who had apparently sat down with the sheet in front of him, then turned and had the knife driven into his chest. Presumably he had known that someone else was in the room, but had not expected to be attacked.

'So he was going to write something,' Dawlish said, in a faraway voice. He looked speculatively at the breast pocket. He could not make up his mind whether to search the body before the police arrived. It would be noticed, in all likelihood, and was it worth antagonising the authorities?

Tim caught his attention with a sharp: 'What's that?'

Dawlish followed the direction of the pointing finger. Beneath a small bureau was a screwed-up piece of paper. Tim bent to recover it, then straightened it out.

'I—' he began, and then his voice trailed off.

Urgently Dawlish took the paper from him.

It was a typewritten letter, addressed to *Linda Keen*! It asked her to call on Lamb that evening, about half-past ten. Something in the curtness of the wording suggested that it was more than a request; it was an order.

'Well, well,' said Dawlish, in a tone of complete astonishment. 'Call The Pines, Tim.'

The piece of paper he now held was evidence that Linda had been in this room since Lamb had returned. If her prints were on it, it would be almost conclusive proof. At least he could keep that from the police until later, but there was more cause for alarm; she might have touched other things, and thus give away her presence to the police. He moved towards the table and looked at the polished surface, peering closely. He thought he could see where a duster had been rubbed over it, in hurried, circular motions.

He examined the door; that, too, had been recently polished. So had a table by the wall, a small bookcase, and several other articles of furniture.

He went into the hall, and glanced at the front door. There was no evidence that the lock had been forced. He stood with his hands thrust deep in his pockets, frowning, when Tim called out:

'O.K., Pat! . . . Hallo, Fel, Pat wants you.'

Dawlish hurried to the telephone. There was a note of alarm in Felicity's voice, and Dawlish was prepared for what came.

'Pat, I've been ringing the flat, but got no answer. Linda has disappeared.'

'Since when?'

'She went to her room soon after supper, saying she had a headache,' said Felicity. 'There was a 'phone call for her about an hour ago, and I went to call her—but she wasn't there!'

'Bed slept in?' asked Dawlish.

'Apparently not,' said Felicity.

'I think she left of her own free will,' said Dawlish. 'Do you know if she got a letter by the afternoon post?'

'Yes,' said Felicity. 'I met the postman, and gave it to her myself.'

'Hum,' said Dawlish. 'Well, go back to sleep, and say nothing about it. In fact you'd better forget the whole thing. I fully expect her to turn up before morning, so don't worry, don't question her if she does come back and persuade Simon to say nothing, too.'

'You sound very mysterious,' said Felicity, soberly. 'I wonder if you know how very frustrating it is to be given one bite of the apple!'

'That depends on the apple,' said Dawlish cryptically. 'Now be a good girl, and hop back to bed.' He rang off.

Tim was still staring at the letter.

'She's been here all right,' Dawlish said. 'The quicker I can see her the better.'

'What about the police?'

'You've gone police conscious all of a sudden, haven't you?' asked Dawlish, with a grin. 'Cast your mind back, Tim. You say that Lamb left Layer Street this morning without even a week-end bag. Was he carrying anything at all?'

Tim frowned. 'I don't think—oh, yes, he did! It was a small black brief case. A very small one, certainly not large enough for a change of clothes. Why?'

'It isn't here,' said Dawlish, simply.

'He might have put it into another room,' Tim suggested.

'I doubt it.'

Together they searched the flat, but the case was not to be found. Dawlish made sure that both his and Tim's fingerprints were wiped clean, and then at long last he telephoned Trivett at his home.

Trivett was remarkably alert for a man awakened in the middle of the night. He promised to come round at once, and he was at the flat by half-past two. Soon afterwards, a team arrived from Scotland Yard with a camera, fingerprint equipment, and other oddments. A police surgeon was on the way.

'Glossing over the fact that you got inside without a key,' said Trivett, with an air of casual interest, 'why did you come, Pat?'

'To talk to Lamb.'

'Why?'

'Because I was told—in circumstances that made it extremely likely to be the truth—that Lamb was responsible for the attack on Keen.'

'Where is your informer now?'

'I won't lose him, don't worry; and I don't think there'll be any trouble with this one.' As he spoke, Dawlish wondered if he had, after all, been wise to leave Crabb alone at his flat. He was suddenly anxious to go and see the man. Trivett, for all his leniency, could hardly be expected to accept with equilibrium the possible disappearance or demise of yet a second prisoner.

'We'd better have him,' said Trivett.

'I suppose so. Look here, Bill—come round to the flat when you've finished here, will you? And—er—if you find anything of interest in Lamb's pockets, bring it with you.'

'You've probably got all that's of interest in your own pocket,' said Trivett, drily.

'For once you're wrong,' said Dawlish, virtuously. 'We left that entirely to you!'

As quickly as they could, Dawlish and Tim returned to the Brook Street flat. Dawlish was more relieved than he would have liked Trivett to think, to find Crabb sitting just where they had left him.

Tim dived into the kitchen to make a pot of tea, while Dawlish turned to Crabb. He told him that the police would soon be arriving, and would want to interview him.

'You'll have a chance of turning Queen's Evidence,' he said, 'and I will do all I can to make sure that you're leniently treated— on one condition.'

Crabb looked up, as if, expecting little of life, he saw these expectations again fulfilled.

'What's that?'

'That you don't tell the police what I'm now going to ask you,' said Dawlish. 'Be as frank as you can otherwise, indeed, your statement will sound much more convincing if you tell the truth about your share in it. Do you understand?'

'Yes,' Crabb said. He sipped the tea which Tim had handed to him, and drew at a cigarette.

'Right! Now for the question which is strictly hush-hush. How well did Lamb know Linda Keen?'

Crabb said: 'I don't know much about it. Only that they were once friendly. I think there was a quarrel.'

'Did he use pressure on her?'

'How do you mean?'

'Did he know anything against her?' asked Dawlish, patiently.

Crabb shrugged.

'As I said, all I know is that there was some kind of a row, then she stopped coming to see him.'

'How long had they known each other?'

'About six months.'

'Hum,' said Dawlish. 'Every starting point in this business seems to date back six months.' He lit another cigarette, and poured out more tea. 'Did Lamb make arrangements to see her during the last day or two, do you know?'

Crabb shrugged.

'Couldn't say. He could see her as often as he wanted to at Hindhead, couldn't he?'

'I suppose so,' said Dawlish.

It was a negative result, but all, at the moment, he was likely to get. Before long, Trivett turned up with a sergeant. He assured Dawlish that nothing at all had been found at the flat which offered any clue. He seemed disappointed, and more than a little suspicious, until Dawlish told him about the missing brief case.

'So you think the murderer took it?' asked Trivett.

'Probably.' Dawlish stifled a yawn, and then grinned apologetically. 'Sorry, Bill, but I'm about to drop! Crabb's in the other room. I've promised him that you'll give him a square deal, and take Queen's Evidence from him.'

'We'd take Queen's Evidence from the Devil himself, on this case,' said Trivett.

'So it's worrying you as much as that,' said Dawlish. 'You aren't prepared to tell me what you think it's all about, I suppose?'

'I can't,' said Trivett, briefly.

The fact that the affair was connected with some mysterious hush-hush business troubled Dawlish, but it was not long after Trivett had gone that he went to bed, and he was soon asleep. He was anxious that he or Tim should relieve Ted fairly early, and set an alarm clock for 6.30. That would give him two hours sleep. He slept for five, before he was disturbed by Tim, who came into the room with a cup of tea.

Dawlish struggled up, glancing at the clock.

'Good Lord! If I slept through that alarm—'

'You didn't,' said Tim, 'I came in and put the catch down.' He pulled the curtains back with the mock servility of a stage valet. 'I went over to see Ted,' he added, 'and found him drinking tea with Belle Lennox. She seemed happy enough now that it's daylight, so we left her.'

'Then where's Ted?'

'In bed—where I'm going, unless you've planned another scene of Sherlock Holmesian drama for me.'

'Turn in, old chap, by all means—I'll give you a call before I go down to The Pines.'

Finishing a light breakfast, Dawlish first telephoned the hospital at Haslemere, and was assured that Keen was still unconscious; then he telephoned The Pines. Linda answered him. She sounded fresh and lively, and promised to fetch Felicity at once. He was frowning when Felicity came.

'Well, how are tricks?' asked Dawlish.

'Not too bad,' said Felicity, in a low voice. 'They're in the kitchen, so I can talk fairly freely. She was back soon after six o'clock. She hasn't said anything about going out, and Simon hasn't said anything about it either. The whole atmosphere is much brighter down here, as if some strain has gone. Do you know where she went?'

'I'm not sure,' said Dawlish, mendaciously. He added: 'Oh—there's one other thing, my poppet! That telephone for her that caused all the bother last night—who was it from, do you know?'

'I only know that it was a man's voice, and that it came from London,' Felicity told him.

'Oh, well,' said Dawlish. 'I'll be with you for tea, I hope. Good

Lord, I'm late! Sorry, sweet, I've an appointment for eleven o'clock. 'Bye!'

It was then half-past ten, and he was anxious to get to Layer Street in order to be present when Bland arrived for his second attempt to get information from Marion. He wrote a brief note to Ted and Tim saying where he had gone, and left the flat at twenty minutes to eleven. The only way he could hope to get to Layer Street by eleven o'clock was by taxi, but he was unlucky, and it was nearly ten minutes before he got one. At five past eleven the cab turned into Layer Steet—and, parked outside Number 18, was Bland's Lanchester.

'Oh, well,' said Dawlish, philosophically.

He walked briskly up to the gate, and then, alert and startled, saw Marion running from the open front door.

CHAPTER NINETEEN

BLACK-EYE FOR BLAND

Marion pulled up, gasping for breath.

'Thank—goodness—you're here!' she said, and grabbing his arm hurried him back to the house.

As they entered the hall, Dawlish heard the furious shuffle of fighting bodies, followed by a protesting cry in a woman's voice—*Belle's* voice.

The din was coming from the room in which he had first seen Marion. The door was ajar. He pushed it open—and then Bland, reeling under a punch from Graham, fell heavily against him. Dawlish pushed him to one side, for Graham was coming forward, fists clenched, a glint of fury in his eyes. Dawlish caught his arm. He appeared to be unhurt. Bland, on the other hand, breathing stertorously, his eyes closed, had fallen to the floor.

'I think—' began Dawlish.

'Get out of my way!' snapped Graham. He had completely lost all self-control as he aimed a swinging blow which sent the large man reeling against a chair.

By the fireplace, staring in wide-eyed alarm, hovered Belle. Marion now stood in the doorway.

'Father—' she began.

'Move away!' cried Graham. He bent over Bland, and, showing surprising strength, hoisted the man to his feet.

Bland was conscious; his flickering eyes and the expression on his face proved that. With a surprising cunning he wriggled free—and for the first time Dawlish saw him when he was roused, when the naked evil of which he was capable showed and the civilised veneer, so carefully assumed, had completely gone.

In his right hand was an automatic.

'I've warned you, Graham—'

'You fool!' roared Dawlish.

He did not think that it would be any more use to reason with Bland than with Graham. As Bland fired the automatic he pushed the other to one side. The shot passed between them. Next moment Dawlish seized Bland's wrists, exerting such pressure that the gun dropped to the floor. A second shot came from it, and thudded into the wainscoting.

'What do you want—to be sentenced for murder?' snapped Dawlish. He picked up the gun and dropped it into his pocket.

Bland stared at him with unveiled hostility. Silence fell upon the room—until slowly the malignance faded from Bland's eyes. He straightened his coat, and put a hand to his tie.

'Thank you, Major Dawlish,' he said. 'Thank you. I am afraid I lost my self-control.' He glanced at Graham with a hard, malevolent stare, bowed to Marion, then turned with an odd dignity; he did not look at Belle.

He went out.

Graham's fury seemed to have spent itself. Dawlish followed Bland, without interference.

'You'd better bathe your face,' Dawlish suggested.

'I shall do so later,' said Bland. His words, from between swollen lips, were hard to distinguish. 'Dawlish, I beg you to take this seriously. If you have any influence with Graham, tell him it will serve no purpose to delay his decision. Greater powers than I are at work—and far, far greater powers than Graham.'

'Such as the police,' murmured Dawlish.

'The *police*!' sneered Bland. 'What do I—' He broke off, and turned away again. That odd dignity was still with him as he staggered to his car. Before reaching it, however, he turned once again. 'Major Dawlish, I am sorry that we are on opposite sides. I appreciate your help and your fairness. I would like you to perform a service for me.'

'Certainly, if it's possible.'

'Tell my—tell Belle that I bear no umbrage. I understand what has happened. I make full allowance for human failings. Tell her that if she wishes to marry this man, she *must* make him do my bidding. Otherwise—'

He stepped into the car.

Dawlish watched the Lanchester drive off, and then he heard footsteps coming from the house. It was Marion.

'What on earth led up to this?' he asked.

'About fifteen minutes before Bland turned up, Father arrived quite unexpectedly—with Belle.' There was something in her manner which told Dawlish that she had thawed, if only a little, towards the older woman. 'They went into the room next to the drawing-room. There is a communicating door, and it was ajar. Bland came next, and started to talk as he had done last night. Father heard him and burst in. Then Bland *ordered* Belle out of the house. I hadn't realised before what there was between them. She *is* his mistress, isn't she?'

'I believe she was, once,' said Dawlish.

'He appeared to think she still is,' said Marion, with a catch in her breath. 'I thought Father would go mad! It must have been an awful shock to him. Then Belle—then Belle said, very simply, that she was going to do all she could to help my father, what-ever the consequences. I don't know why,' added Marion, in a wondering voice, 'but by saying that she went up a great deal in my estimation. I could see that Bland was not normal. I could tell what an effort it was for her to defy him. It was almost as if she knew he had the power of life and death over her and yet she did not flinch or hesitate.'

'No,' said Dawlish. 'Belle is a strong-willed woman.'

Marion said: 'Bland called her foul names. Father turned on him. That's all, really.'

'And quite enough,' said Dawlish. 'Did Bland make any offer for The Grange?'

'No, he didn't get as far as that.'

'Oh, well,' said Dawlish, 'we'll see what his next trick is.'

He was by no means sure what kind of a reception he would get from Graham, but this was an opportunity for frank talking which was not likely to occur again.

He found Graham waiting for him. Belle was with him.

'I'm afraid I butted in,' murmured Dawlish.

Graham said, in a stilted voice: 'I must thank you for your intervention, Major Dawlish. It might have been much more serious had you not arrived. Do you wish to see me?'

'Yes,' said Dawlish. 'About several things.' He smiled at Belle. 'First and foremost—*are* you thinking of selling your house?'

'No, I am *not*!' said Graham sharply.

'Bland thinks you are.'

'I am not interested in what Bland thinks,' said Graham. 'I have received offers, as I told you, but nothing would persuade me to sell. If you are a would-be purchaser—'

'Not I!' said Dawlish, with a grin. 'I'm after something much easier to run!' His manner seemed to create a lighter atmo-sphere. 'You don't know why Bland wants it, I suppose?'

'I have no idea.'

Belle interrupted.

'I have told Raymond what happened last night, Major Dawlish, and how deeply I am indebted to you. If you want to talk about anything resulting from that, I am quite sure that Raymond will be glad to help.'

'There isn't a lot of point in going over last night,' said Dawlish. 'Oh ' he hesitated, aiming at creating the greatest sensation— 'there's one item of bad news, I'm afraid.' He paused again, noting the way they all watched him. 'Lamb was murdered last night,' he said.

Both the women gave involuntary exclamations, while Graham took a short step forward.

'*Lamb!*' he exclaimed.

'Murdered in cold blood,' said Dawlish. 'By whom, I don't know. As you were a neighbour, Sir Raymond, the police will probably ask for your help.'

'I—' began Graham. He broke off, groping for cigarettes. The room was quiet for a moment, until the scrape of a match broke the silence. 'I can hardly believe it,' he went on. 'I saw him only yesterday morning. He—'

'On what business?' Dawlish asked.

'The sale of The Pines,' said Graham.

'Ah,' murmured Dawlish. 'The police will probably be very curious about your anxiety to buy that house.'

'I have nothing to hide from the police,' said Graham. 'Lamb and I were in full agreement. We did not want the district spoiled. Why was he killed, do you know?'

'No,' said Dawlish. *Had* Belle told Graham of her suspicions of Lamb? 'Presumably in connection with this business.'

'I suppose so. Belle was telling me—' Graham's voice trailed off. He drew hard at his cigarette. 'Major Dawlish,' he went on in a level voice, 'it appears that you have been forced into a some-what unenviable position—a knowledge of the private affairs of both myself and my daughter. I am sorry you have been trou-bled by them, but as you have, and as you appear to have a wide knowledge of the mystery in which they are connected, I would appreciate your help.'

'In what particular way?'

'Lamb, apparently, had some purpose in attacking the young man to whom Marion is engaged. Do you know *why* the attack was considered necessary?'

'No,' said Dawlish, 'but I can guess. Let's be wholly frank, shall we? I think that Lamb was a tool in Bland's hands. I think Bland arranged for Belle to work on you, and for Barry to work on your daughter. He made two bad moves there. I think Barry Keen rebelled, and thus got himself into trouble with Bland, hence the attack. I think that Lamb was in a position to betray Bland, and was probably killed because of that. He pretended to be a friend of yours, Graham, but he was working against you. Bland told your daughter last night that he was quite sure that you were considering selling The Grange. I assumed that he got his information from Lamb. Were there any grounds for it?'

He would not have been surprised if Graham had uttered another denial. Instead, after a long pause, the man said slowly:

'I did at one time contemplate selling The Grange. Since then, however, I have been able to avoid the financial crisis which alone made the thought of a sale possible.'

'A change of fortune,' murmured Dawlish.

Graham said sharply: 'A natural one, and not altogether unexpected. Some of my holdings have recovered after they were much below par. I am telling you this because I owe you a considerable debt, Major Dawlish, but—'

'I won't discuss it with the police,' said Dawlish, 'but you will, if you are wise.'

'What do you mean?'

'Look here,' said Dawlish. 'Lamb organised an attack on Keen—Marion's fiancé. Lamb knew you were at one time in financial difficulties. The police *might* think you had a motive for killing Lamb.'

'That's utter nonsense,' snapped Graham.

'Not really,' Dawlish insisted. 'You must see that there's a very real chance of suspicion. You may have had a personal reason, or you may have been actuated by the highest motives—of saving your daughter's fiancé from serious difficulties.'

'I know nothing about him!'

'I'm not giving you my reasoned opinion,' said Dawlish. 'I am trying to make you understand what the police might think. When did you leave The Grange?'

Graham snapped: 'That is my business!'

'The police may think it's theirs.'

'Quite immaterial if they do,' said Graham loftily. 'I am not entirely without friends, who—'

Dawlish broke in with a flash of irritation.

'If you think that friends in high places will make the slightest difference to the treatment you receive from the police, you are making a big mistake. Obviously you left The Grange last night. You could have been to Lamb's place, and killed him.'

'Was he killed in London or Hindhead?' asked Graham.

'London.'

Graham said: 'Perhaps this information will scotch your absurd suspicions, Major Dawlish. I was at my club last night. I was in my room from eleven o'clock until this morning, when I was called at seven. I have no doubt that the club's staff will corroborate my statement.'

But why, thought Dawlish, had Graham gone to his club, instead of coming home?

Aloud, he said smiling: 'That's good! It makes it much easier if one remembers time and place, in an emergency of this kind.' He turned to go, Graham walking with him along the hall.

He said suddenly: 'Have you had any further news of Barry Keen?'

'He is still unconscious, but out of danger I believe,' said Dawlish. 'I telephoned an inquiry this morning.'

'Do you know the young man?'

'No, only his sister, for whom I have a very high regard.'

'I do not know her well enough to form an opinion,' said Graham, 'but I am naturally anxious to do everything I can to promote my daughter's happiness. This young man, her brother, appears to be in some trouble with the police. That may not be entirely his own fault, of course. Major Dawlish—' He paused for a moment, and then went on: 'Because of him I do not propose to tell the police of the incident here today. And now I must thank you again for your help—you have been more than good.'

'Not at all,' said Dawlish. 'Goodbye.'

As he walked out of the gate, he saw a car turn into the road. It was a green Morris, and Trivett was at the wheel. Dawlish waited until the car pulled up outside Graham's house, and then went thoughtfully on to Brook Street.

Here he discussed the situation with Ted and Tim, agreeing that Tim should watch Graham and Ted keep an eye on Belle, before he, himself, set out for The Pines.

He drove down at a good speed. No one followed him. He had plenty of time for reflection, and was even able to spare a little for enjoyment of the countryside which was bathed in all the glory of early summer. It was hard to associate murder and sudden death, lurking evil and a mystery of sinister importance, with England on such a day. He even found himself humming as he took the Hindhead Road.

A policeman was at the gate of The Pines. He saluted respectfully and Dawlish answered with a broad grin, but the sight of him disturbed Dawlish. For the first time he realised that the police, on duty all night, probably knew that Linda had been away from the house.

CHAPTER TWENTY

THE BLACK BRIEF CASE

As he reached the top of the drive he heard Linda laughing. There was an unaffected gaiety about it which astonished him. The front door was open, and he went in, walking quietly down the planks towards the kitchen. Another burst of laughter greeted him as he reached the kitchen door.

'Pat!' Felicity leapt up from her chair and came towards him. 'You're earlier than I expected.'

'Hence the unbecoming levity,' said Dawlish, with a grin. 'Has someone offered you a fortune for The Pines, Simon?'

'Not yet,' said Simon, 'but it's spring and we're young—or youngish. And even the afflicted can have enough of gloom. Oh—there's one thing you don't know. Barry's come round.'

'And I've been allowed to see him!' exclaimed Linda.

'Splendid!' said Dawlish.

It was not so easy to pretend to be equally lighthearted. It seemed to him that something more than spring, and being young, was responsible for lifting the gloom from Simon and Linda. He did not think he was wrong in believing that Simon was incapable of putting on an act. The brightness was real enough, Dawlish thought.

That probably meant that Linda had told him where she had been, and what she had done.

He was glad when he and Felicity were able to get up to their room. He kissed her, lifting her high off the floor.

'Pat!' she cried. 'Put me down!'

'*Quite* the most beautiful woman in England!'

'You'd better look at Linda again,' said Felicity. 'Darling, why is it always so good to see you?'

He lowered her gently on to the bed, where she sat, her legs tucked under her.

'Well, what's been happening?'

'Ah, ha, I thought that was coming,' said Felicity, laughing. 'And as a reward for being so transparent, I'll tell you. I did exactly as you said, expecting to be met this morning with dark looks and suspicious innuendo. Instead, what a surprise! Both as lively as crickets, hugging some stupendously happy secret to their bosoms!'

'I hardly think crickets do have secrets,' said Dawlish, 'let alone bosoms.'

'As you're not a cricket, I hardly think you're in a position to know,' said Felicity coldly.

'Peace, woman, I'll take your word for it. Linda hasn't confided in you, of course?'

'Not by as much as a word,' said Felicity.

'H'm. When you saw her come in this morning, had she got anything with her?'

'A smallish case,' said Felicity.

'Ah, Did the police see her?'

'I don't know,' said Felicity. 'I rather expected them to come and question her, especially now that Barry's regained consciousness. Strange that Linda doesn't seem worried about that any more.'

'Queer show altogether,' said Dawlish.

'Well, what have *you* been doing?'

'Oh, a little here and a little there,' said Dawlish, airily. 'You don't want to worry your pretty head—'

'Patrick!'

'Yes, dear,' said Dawlish, meekly.

He told her what had happened. He enjoyed the telling. It enabled him to see events in a better perspective. The narrative took half an hour, and they had been upstairs an hour when there was a tap at the door.

Linda entered; her brightness in no way diminished.

'Just off to the shop,' she said. 'You'll keep an eye on Simon for me, won't you?'

'We'll watch him,' promised Dawlish.

It struck him as an odd request; she had never worried in the past about leaving Simon on his own. It might have been a hint that he wanted to talk to Dawlish, but if so he was not taking it. As soon as she had gone he stood up.

'Now, Felicity, a little wifely tact is called for. Tell Simon I'm having a bath, or anything that occurs to you.'

Quickly he slipped across the landing to Linda's room. He saw at once the two small suitcases near the wardrobe; both proved to be empty.

He started to search thoroughly in the quest for the black brief case, but found nothing. He stood back, frowning. There was no certainty that she had brought it from Lamb's flat, but he would bet his last half crown that she had.

He moved the pillows from the bed and lifted the mattress, but the case was not there.

He pulled up a stool and looked on top of the wardrobe; but nothing lay on the smooth, blank surface. He was beginning to think that he was wrong, when he remembered that he had not moved the cushions from a Victorian armchair.

Without much hope, he lifted first the top, and then the under one.

The case was there.

There was no doubt that it was Lamb's. His initials, P.L., were clearly stamped, and on the inside of the flap was a card, giving his London address. Dawlish was not surprised to find the case empty.

He glanced at his watch; it was nearly half an hour since Linda had left, and she would soon be back. He tucked the case under his coat and ran downstairs. In the garden, Simon, his whole being wreathed in contentment, was wielding a short-handed hoe. Dawlish hesitated, wondering whether to tackle them individually, or together. Linda made up his mind for him, for almost at once she joined them. One thing seemed certain: she would not be so carefree if murder was on her conscience.

Unless, he thought grimly, he was mistaken about her character. He wondered a little uneasily whether he had not taken the sincerity of this couple rather too much for granted.

Linda put a hand on Simon's chair, and pushed it into the kitchen. They were both laughing.

Dawlish said abruptly: 'Have you seen Lamb lately?'

The words acted like a cold douche. Both faces grew suddenly dark.

'What do you mean?' demanded Linda, sharply.

'Come, it was a natural question—'

'It was not! Why did you mention Lamb's name then?'

Dawlish looked from her to Simon. There was tension there, not unlike that he had seen when he had first met them. He did not need any further evidence to be assured that they knew Lamb was dead; yet as far as Dawlish knew, the information had not reached them officially.

He said, easily: 'You're right, there was an association of ideas. Where did you get Lamb's brief case, Linda? And what have you done with the papers you took from it?'

She stood, unsmiling, her arms rigid by her side, saying nothing.

Dawlish allowed the silence to go on just so long, then continued:

'You know that if the police discover that you went to his flat, you will probably be charged with the murder. Or hasn't that occurred to you?'

Linda said passionately: 'I did not kill him. Oh, I know he is dead, I know he was murdered, and I'm glad—do you understand that? I'm *glad*!'

'Didn't you realise that this house is under police surveillance, and that in all probability you have been seen leaving it?'

'I used a certain amount of commonsense,' Linda said coldly. 'No one knows I was away last night—except you and Felicity and Simon. If the police ever learn, we shall know who told them.'

'A threat which leaves me entirely unshaken. Now listen to me. It's easy to say you didn't kill him. But the fact remains that from the time you knew he was dead, you have been more carefree than I have ever known you. The watching policemen won't fail to include that in their report. They aren't fools, you know.'

Linda said: 'There's no need for them to know that I was in London!'

'The point is, is there any reason why they shouldn't? Why did you go, Linda? And what did you find to make you so happy?'

'I don't *have* to answer you,' she said sharply.

'No,' said Dawlish. 'No, there's no compulsion. But you asked me to come down here to help, you know. I've come across a number of strange things, and there is obviously some serious crime in the making. I mean to see the end of it, and I mean to help the police, if necessary. Why did you go?'

Harcourt exclaimed: 'Are you threatening to tell the police if Linda doesn't tell you?'

'Yes,' said Dawlish, simply.

Linda flared up.

'You say that, after promising to help us in every way you could!'

'At no time did I agree to condone murder,' said Dawlish.

'I didn't kill Lamb!'

'You're making that very hard to believe.'

'Of all the damnable things to imply—' began Harcourt.

'Now be sensible!' snapped Dawlish, looking suddenly angry. 'Murder *is* murder. There might be a sound reason for concealing the fact of Linda's visit from the police, but there is none at all for concealing it from me. The choice is yours,' he added abruptly, 'you'd better think it over.'

He turned on his heel and left them, searching the garden until he found Felicity. At sight of his expression, her eyebrows rose.

'They're being stubborn,' Dawlish said. 'I think I chose the wrong method of tackling them. They've adopted an attitude of injured innocence and blunt denial without deigning to explain. Even the threat of going to the police hasn't moved them.'

'Why on earth—' Felicity began.

'That's just the question,' said Dawlish. 'Why on earth should they suddenly keep me out of their confidences? The odd thing,' he added, 'is that I find it hard to believe that she *did* kill him. And if she didn't, why is she so anxious not to let me know about it?'

Felicity had the wifely intuition to see that though an answer was sought, it was not sought from her. Though bursting with solutions, she watched silently, with admirable restraint, as he filled his pipe.

Suddenly he snapped his fingers.

'Got it!' he exclaimed, his eyes blazing. 'My sweet, we've been had for a couple of mugs. We were fobbed off with only part of the story, and have never been told the real reason why Simon sent for us. Oh, they've strung us along very cleverly indeed, and I *think* I know what's what!'

His excitement was contagious.

'Don't keep it to yourself!' cried Felicity. 'I—'

The crack of a shot sounded loud above her words; in front of Dawlish's eyes, she staggered. She spun round, gasping, the colour suddenly drained from her face. He caught her as she fell, and as another bullet passed over his head.

CHAPTER TWENTY-ONE

DAWLISH FEELS LIKE MURDER

There was something warm and wet on his fingers as he touched Felicity. He saw her eyes open, and read the pain in them. With a movement of anguish he swung her from the ground and dived among the nearest trees. A third bullet struck the ground a yard in front of him. Then he was safely under cover.

Men were shouting; a police whistle sounded. Footsteps sounded near the house, and he heard Linda call out.

'Who was it? Who—'

Dawlish satisfied that the immediate danger had gone, turned from the trees and hurried towards the house. The police could search for the sharp-shooter. Linda met him, her face pale.

'Let me pass,' he said savagely.

She turned and hurried ahead of him. Simon appeared at the front door, his face showing his alarm.

'I—' he began, then added quickly: 'Use my room.'

Dawlish strode forward. Felicity was still conscious, but there was a deep fear in him, that she was seriously hurt.

'I'll telephone for a doctor,' Harcourt said, and spun the wheels of his chair.

Dawlish laid Felicity on the bed. The blood was on his sleeve and cuff, and had spread from her shoulder. She did not try to speak, but closed her eyes, as if the pain was too much to bear. He scarcely realised what had happened with such bewildering suddenness. In one moment the affair had ceased being a problem to be settled with detachment; instead it had become intensely personal. He felt a burning rage which showed in his eyes and his grimly set mouth.

Linda came in, pushing him gently but authoritatively aside.

He let her take over, recognising that professional competence was of greater importance than all his love and anguish. He stood a little way off, watching the woman's deft fingers, and seeing the pallor of Felicity's cheeks.

There was absolutely nothing he could do. What he had seen a hundred times without flinching, he saw now for the first time with horror. *Felicity's* blood. He did not think that either Linda or Harcourt knew who had fired. His animosity for them had gone; he thanked God that she was at hand, and could work so efficiently and with such detachment. She bandaged Felicity with strips of a sheet, winding them round and round and drawing them tightly.

Why didn't the doctor come? His thoughts were chaotic, his anger now fastening on the doctor; *why* wasn't he here? He glared furiously out of the window. A car had come into sight along the drive, followed by an ambulance.

Quietly, efficiently, Felicity was taken away. As the stretcher was carried with expert skill through the door, the doctor turned to him.

'I think I would stay here, Major Dawlish, if I were you. I will telephone you as soon as I have made my examination.'

'I'll do that,' said Dawlish. 'Thanks.'

It was strange, Dawlish thought a little bitterly, how in any physical crisis those we love most in the world were delivered up to strangers, and, indeed, considered by them to be imperilled by that very love.

'I will give her a shot of morphia in the ambulance, if I think it wise. Don't worry, now,' the doctor continued gently. He rested a hand on Dawlish's arm, and then hurried out, to drive immediately behind the ambulance. Dawlish watched them out of sight, and then turned and looked at Felicity's blood-soaked blouse.

Linda came in; she was carrying a tea tray.

'Will you have a lacing of whisky?' she asked.

'No thanks,' said Dawlish. He was grateful for the tea. As he sipped it, Harcourt came along. Both of them looked abashed—ashamed, perhaps, was the better word. Dawlish looked at them evenly, until Harcourt broke the quiet.

'Saying sorry is useless, I know. But—we do appreciate that—that this is the result of you answering our appeal. We feel responsible. We—'

'Well?'

Harcourt looked at Linda, and then threw up his hands helplessly.

'We have decided to tell you what you want to know, though we thought at the time it would be wiser to keep it to ourselves. Still, Linda—you tell him.'

Linda began to speak with an air of truth and sincerity. She had, she said, received an order from Lamb to see him at his London flat. She had been there before, several times, and was aware of the fact that he worked for Bland, and that he knew something to her brother's discredit. She had obeyed him, because she had been afraid of what he would tell the police about Barry. As she was nearing his flat she saw a man entering it, leaving the door open. She followed him, expecting it to be Lamb. The man started to search the desk, and seeing that he was not Lamb, she waited in another room.

Soon afterwards, Lamb had arrived.

He had not sounded surprised to see the other man. They had talked for a few minutes, while she had waited, afraid of showing herself before the stranger went. When she heard the door closing, she expected Lamb to appear; but the flat was silent. She went into the room, and saw that he was dead.

By his side was a brief case.

'I had the letter telling me to go there in my hand, and I remember now that I screwed it up and threw it away. I picked up the brief case and looked inside—'

Harcourt broke in, a little uncertainly.

'Dawlish, we haven't been absolutely frank with you. Oh, we've told you the truth all right, but not enough of it. The reason, the whole point of the intrigue, is that this house is on valuable land—not for building,' he added, 'but for—'

'Mineral content,' said Dawlish, harshly. 'What is it? Oil?'

'Yes,' said Linda, breathlessly. 'We thought it might be, and in that brief case we found papers confirming it. Inside was a prospector's report, made while the Government had taken over the house. Lamb had it. No wonder they wanted to buy the house! Why, it is worth a fortune!'

'The knowledge of which,' said Dawlish drily, 'you were disinclined to trust with me.'

'It—it seemed wiser to keep it to ourselves,' said Harcourt, awkwardly. 'When we wrote to you, we didn't know about it, but thought there might be a chance of tin or lead. Both were found near here once, and there are still the old huts where the miners worked and sometimes lived. Then Linda heard Lamb talking to someone—'

'Let's forget it,' said Dawlish. 'If there is oil here in any quantity, it's enough to cause all the shindy.' He paused. 'But if the authorities found some here, why didn't they go down for it?'

'Don't ask me,' said Harcourt, helplessly. 'Here's the report.'

Dawlish glanced through it. It was a detailed surveyor's report, signed by two people with strings of letters after their names, and it left the reader in no doubt as to the value of the oil deposits.

Much, now, was easy to understand.

Even the couple in front of him could hardly be blamed for their secrecy. Their sudden cheerfulness was easily explained, and had a two-fold reason. Oil meant that money troubles were behind them, and Lamb's death, that anxiety over Barry was at an end. Dawlish handed the report back.

'If you're wise you'll tell the police as soon as they come out here again. Hall, I mean. Tell him everything. They'll find out that Linda was at Lamb's place, there isn't any doubt of that.'

'I suppose you're right,' muttered Harcourt.

'I'm sure I am.'

The telephone bell rang.

Dawlish sped past them and lifted the receiver in a flash, listening with a thumping heart.

'I think we shall have her all right in a few weeks,' the doctor assured him. 'The shoulder blade was broken, but not so badly that we can't mend it, and we've got the bullet. There is no cause for alarm, no cause at all.'

'Thank God!'

'Yes, indeed. An eighth of an inch to the left—Well, well. Come and see her at the hospital some time after nine o'clock. You can have five minutes. She will be round from the anaesthetic by then.'

'I'll be there,' said Dawlish.

He replaced the receiver, surprised to find that his hands were trembling, and that even his legs felt none too steady.

CHAPTER TWENTY-TWO

WORK!

As he turned away from the telephone, Dawlish caught sight of one of the policemen, and it occurred to him for the first time as odd that they had not come to speak to him after the shooting. Now that Felicity was off the danger list and his mind freed of terror, he could concentrate more clearly on the answer to the riddle. *Oil*—it seemed the obvious one. It was cleverly done—Bland, working under the guise of a building company, had made it appear nothing more than land speculation for opportunist building.

A car turned into the drive, and he recognised the local Inspector, Hall. Dawlish heard Harcourt waylay him. Their voices, intermingling, seemed to go on for a long time.

It was half an hour before he heard footsteps.

Hall came into the room, with a faint smile. He was glad that Mrs. Dawlish was out of danger, he said. He was also glad that Major Dawlish had persuaded Harcourt and Linda Keen to tell everything they knew about the mystery, and about the murder of Lamb.

'Are you making a charge against Linda?' asked Dawlish.

'Hardly,' said Hall. 'We haven't reached that stage. In any case, the affair is in the controlling hands of Trivett.'

'H'mm,' said Dawlish. 'In other words, it's a Home Office show.' He tapped a cigarette on his thumb-nail. 'Well, I'm no longer interested in what is behind it. I am interested only in who shot my wife, who killed Lamb, and attacked Barry Keen. Have you any answers?'

'Not yet, I'm afraid,' said Hall, 'except that we know the men whom you—'

'Tools,' said Dawlish, briefly. 'We want the higher game.' He felt a cold, dispassionate determination to hunt the gunman down. 'Your men lost him in the grounds, I take it. Did they see in what direction he went?'

'Yes,' said Hall. 'He first made for The Grange. A tall, thin fellow, roughly dressed. Then he cut across by the drive and headed for Lamb's house and the main road. After that he was lost in the trees.'

'Lamb's house,' mused Dawlish. 'Is it occupied?'

'Our men are still there,' said Hall. 'Since his murder we have taken possession. There are only two old servants in residence.'

'So the lanky johnny didn't go into the house,' said Dawlish. 'Could he have cut back and gone to The Grange?'

'No. We have all sides of The Grange watched.'

Dawlish frowned.

'You're making a thorough job of it, aren't you? Is Graham your quarry?'

'I think,' said Hall, portentously, 'that Sir Raymond Graham is in considerable danger of being murdered.'

'Ah,' said Dawlish. 'So you're after Bland.'

'Trivett telephoned to tell us to keep a lookout for him, certainly,' said Hall. 'He's got all the evidence he wants against the gentleman, I think.'

Dawlish nodded thoughtfully.

The point of major interest to him was the fact that Bland was now openly suspected and on the wanted list. Was it possible that Graham had, after all, reported the attack with the gun, and that Trivett had acted on it? Trivett's call at Layer Street that morning might have yielded the necessary results.

Hall took himself off, and Dawlish went up to his room. He felt a sense of frustration which angered him. A tall, thinnish man, roughly-dressed, had fired at Felicity and at him; such a man had visited Lamb, and might be Lamb's murderer. This man Justin, so little known—what was he like to look at?

He hurried downstairs to the telephone.

He remembered the name of the company of which Justin was a director, and he telephoned the *Daily Record*, speaking to a member of the staff. Justin, he learned, was a man of forty-five, wealthy, a good owner—which meant that the conditions at his collieries were excellent—popular with the men and popular with his own kind. To look at? Oh, about six feet, thin, rather ungainly—

'Well, well!' said Dawlish, when he replaced the receiver.

There was a thought troubling him which he could not quite place. Justin—where had he seen the name before? It might be, of course, that he had read it in the Press, and now half-called it to mind, but he could not convince himself that that was all. He had come across the name somewhere in connection with this affair. What names had he seen?

He bounded upstairs, and took from a writing case the documents about the Merrick Building Company which Bland had supplied. He ran through the list of directors—and there, halfway down, was the name Justin. Melford Justin, Esq., V.C., O.B.E., M.P. *The Victoria Cross!* That was in keeping with the whole business, with Bland's conception of a just reward for heroes.

Dawlish felt excited—and then a new thought deflated him. Trivett would not have missed so obvious a connection.

And yet—

Would a man in Justin's position, a wealthy man who, if he were Bland's partner, would be able to call on thugs of the Crabb type, take a personal share in the general violence?

Why not? Dawlish asked himself. Obviously a man of action and courage, he might not trust those who worked for him. He might even have a good reason for wanting to kill Bland. What was it Bland said?

He stood staring out of the window of his room. Bland had talked of greater powers than Graham being behind this business, and he had scoffed at the police. Which great powers were they?

Some great powers had vetoed mention of oil; had determined that the business should be strictly hush-hush. Were they the ones? There was a possible tie-up; and yet Dawlish did not believe that persons in high enough authority to matter would be party to these crimes and to this conspiracy. What would Bland regard as a great power? Money—financial interests. Yes! He had first tried to bribe Dawlish by offering him a sinecure in the post of the Merrick Company's board; and later, with the gift of the house.

For the first time for some days, Dawlish thought of Four Ways. The Owens must now have gone, he assumed, or else were about to go. It was his—whatever he decided, he could not prevent them from taking Bland's money for the house and thus closing the deal.

He heard footsteps in the passage, and Linda's voice calling him.

'Mrs. Owen—you remember her?—says she would like to see you.'

Together they walked downstairs to the drawing-room, Linda leaving him at the door. Mrs. Owen, walking up and down the room agitatedly, greeted him with outstretched hands.

'Can we be overheard in here?'

'Not if we keep our voices low,' said Dawlish. He looked at her, puzzled. 'I hope nothing has gone wrong.'

'*We're* all right,' she said. 'We're nearly ready to leave. Maurice was coming to see you, and then we had a visit from that odious man who tried to buy the place.'

'Bland!' ejaculated Dawlish.

'And he's still at Four Ways,' said Mrs. Owen. 'He came early this morning, and begged us to let him stay there until he could see you. I don't quite know why, but we let him, and there he is. Maurice suggested telephoning, but Bland said that he was quite sure you would come. He seems frightened of the telephone.'

'That's not surprising,' said Dawlish. 'He's wanted by the police for a technical offence.' He grinned.

She looked at him with unexpected seriousness.

'Maurice and I are catching the next train to London, but—well, this seemed important, because he said that your *life* was at stake. He—he gave me this note,' she added.

Why was she so worked up, Dawlish wondered. Was it because Bland had managed to frighten her, or was she being mysterious for the sake of it?

He read the note.

It was written in purple ink, with many flourishes, and it said simply that Dawlish would make a great mistake if he did not come to see him at Four Ways that night. There were no threats, and no attempt at cajolery.

He put the letter in his pocket.

'You can leave it to me, Mrs. Owen,' Dawlish said gently, 'and my warmest thanks for your help in every way.' He led her to the door. 'Don't worry too much about Bland, he isn't as dangerous as he would like to think.'

'Will you go to see him?' asked Mrs. Owen.

'Probably—please tell him that.'

As she said goodbye, he could not help feeling that she was afraid of something which she had not discussed with him. He watched her climb into the small car and go down the drive, and he wondered why she was the messenger, not Maurice Owen. In every way, it was a curious business. He was thinking that he had to go into Haslemere, soon after nine o'clock, to see Felicity. He could go on from there to Four Ways, *if* he thought it wise. Was it a trick? Had the sharpshooting failure encouraged Bland or its sponsor to make this new attempt to trap him?

That brought him to a question which he had evaded since the shooting incident. *Why* had they been so anxious to kill him? It could only be because he had discovered something of importance, something they were afraid he would divulge.

As he stood there, with a soft breeze coming from the grounds, he smelt burning. He stepped into the hall and found Linda and Harcourt by the front door, sniffing the air.

'We were coming to tell you that supper's ready,' said Linda. 'What's on fire?'

From the top floor it was possible to get a good view of the surrounding countryside, and Dawlish bounded up the stairs.

Through one of the web-covered windows of the upper floor he saw a cloud of smoke rising. It came from the direction of The Grange.

No one appeared to be in sight, no one was in the grounds. The fire seemed to gain a greater hold even in the few seconds that Dawlish stood watching. Without wasting any more time, he rushed downstairs. Harcourt was sitting in his wheelchair, grim-faced and inactive.

Dawlish cried out to him to telephone the police and fire station, as he hurried into the grounds. They were strangely deserted.

He remembered the best path to the wall of The Grange grounds. As he ran through the trees, he passed the little well, with the cement lid. The lid was not quite in place. That strange premonition that so unerringly told him that something was wrong caused him to halt and investigate. Exerting all his strength, he shifted the lid a little further to one side.

He saw a man's head.

He realised it was the answer to the strange silence, the desertion of the grounds. Peering down the hole he could see the unconscious bodies of three men in police uniform. Calling on all the energy he possessed he dragged the men free. Though obviously overcome by fumes or gas of some sort their pulses were fairly strong, and Harcourt's telephoned cry for help would be answered shortly. Dawlish felt justified enough to leave the men and continue his urgent rush to The Grange.

It was not quite dark, and reaching the boundary wall he climbed it and dropped to the grassland beyond.

A lurid red glare was coming from The Grange, grotesquely pinpointing the fire fighting unit moving along the drive. It stopped, and men spilled out of it, beginning to unwind their hoses. By now the fire had gained a fairly strong hold. Dawlish remembered with horror the quiet luxury of everything inside, the irreplaceable beauty now being reduced to charred remnants.

There was a more insistent horror. Was anybody still alive in the house?

CHAPTER TWENTY-THREE

COMPLETE DESTRUCTION

'There isn't a thing we can do,' a man said.

Dawlish stood staring at the roaring flames, tongues of which shot out and licked the grass many yards from the building. The house was now nothing but a blazing mass. Now and again the crash of a wall or a floor boomed like a great explosion, and always the flames grew higher and burnt with greater force.

'Get back,' said the man. 'It's not safe here.'

The red glow showed the uniform of the officer in charge of the fire unit. His men were standing helplessly by. Another unit was already at work, pouring water on some outbuildings.

'It must have been started at several places at once,' said the man. 'Was there anyone inside, do you know?'

'There must have been,' said Dawlish sombrely.

His utter powerlessness was the thing which most appalled him, as he stared, his eyes aching from the heat, at the final scene of total destruction.

'Well, anyone who was inside's a gonner,' said the fireman with lugubrious certainty, 'that's sure enough.'

A couple of men were attacking a locked door with an axe.

The inside was illuminated by the red glow from the fire, and appeared to be an empty garage. There were two doors at the far end. Dawlish hurried towards one, the firemen to another. Dawlish pushed his open—

Time seemed to go back; he remembered opening the door of the cupboard under the stairs at The Pines, and finding Felicity, Linda, and Harcourt. This was the same, on a larger scale. A man came from the other room, bearing the same story—that room, too, was filled with servants from The Grange, policemen who had been on duty in the grounds, all lying bound and gagged so that they could do nothing to save The Grange from complete destruction.

'*Why?*' asked Dawlish, helplessly. 'Why?'

Dawlish was back at The Pines. It was being used by the police and the firemen. Linda was kept busy, putting one room and then another at the disposal of the rescued servants, some of whom were suffering severely from shock. All had the same story—of stealthy, unsuspected attack, and then a regained consciousness, to find themselves bound and gagged in the garage.

Trivett arrived from London a little before nine o'clock. He had been on his way, and knew nothing about the fire until he had turned into the drive of The Pines.

Hall, already there, greeted him in the hall, with Dawlish. The local inspector was dazed; it was something quite beyond his comprehension.

'But *why?*' he cried. '*Why?*'

'That's our problem,' said Dawlish. 'Where on earth is Graham?'

Trivett said testily: 'Graham, Miss Lennox, and Marion Graham all left London early this afternoon. They were coming here.'

'They didn't arrive,' Hall said sharply. 'I had a report at half-past six—an hour or so before the fire was first seen. No one had arrived then.'

'I don't think we ought to assume the worst, yet,' said Dawlish easily. 'The main question seems to be—*why*? Perhaps there's a very simple reason: spite, plus.'

'*Very* simple,' said Trivett, sarcastically. 'Plus what?'

'Bland, and probably others, wanted to buy the place for the land only; Graham was determined not to sell. By destroying the house they would increase their chances of buying. Graham presumably knowing nothing of their reason for wanting it.'

'And what might that be?' inquired Trivett.

'Oil,' Dawlish said, patiently.

'Oh,' said Trivett. 'You've got that far. So now you know everything that we do. A relief, really. You might as well know, too, I've a call out for the Grahams and Miss Lennox, not to mention Bland and Justin, the chap from Cardiff.'

'Oh,' said Dawlish, blankly.

'He was seen near here yesterday,' said Trivett, 'about the time that Lamb got to Wales. We've not been idle,' he added, with a touch of complacency, as Linda appeared with tea and sandwiches. 'Thanks very much,' he said warmly. 'I needed that.'

'So Justin could have shot Felicity,' said Dawlish.

'And stabbed Lamb,' said Trivett. 'He was in London.'

'Have you any idea why?'

'No,' said Trivett, 'we haven't got as far as that yet.' He drank his tea with relish. 'I don't like it when a man who is practically unknown suddenly jumps into the limelight as the chief suspect,' he added.

'For once, we're seeing eye to eye,' smiled Dawlish. 'Bill, can I rely on you to be *really* discreet for once?'

Trivett eyed him sharply.

'It depends what about.'

'I think I know where Bland is,' said Dawlish, 'and I think that he might be prepared to tell me the whole truth.'

Trivett put down his cup with great deliberation.

'Now look here, Pat, there are limits to what we can let you do. Crabb should have been turned over to us first, but wasn't, and probably died because of it. Bland must be handed over *at once*.'

Dawlish said: 'Either I'm allowed to work on the business, or I'm not. You can't have it both ways. You may think I'm crazy, but in some fantastic way, Bland has grown *fond* of me.'

'Balderdash,' said Trivett, bluntly.

'It isn't,' said Dawlish. 'He thinks that I have saved his life. He's grateful. I'm almost sure he will tell me the whole story, given the opportunity. If the police question him, I've no doubt at all that he will keep silent. He's the kind of man to picture himself as a martyr, you know. He might be prepared to commit suicide rather than stand trial—suicide, or a glorious death, for some cause in which he believes.'

Both Hall and Trivett looked at him unbelievingly.

'At least you can give me an hour with him,' continued Dawlish. 'What I suggest is that you put a cordon round the house in question, at a good distance at first, and gradually close in. That way, no one can get out. What risk there is I will take.'

'What house?' demanded Trivett.

'Is it a deal?'

'I can't give you permission myself,' said Trivett, 'I haven't the necessary authority.'

'In that case,' said Dawlish, 'I'll try my luck in my own way.'

He had forced the issue, and now appeared disinterested in the outcome. He knew that Trivett could, if he so chose, restrain him by making sure he was not allowed to leave The Pines. The question was whether he had instructions to do so.

'Look here, Pat,' said Trivett, in a reasoning tone, 'if we do let you have a shot at Bland, will you make one promise?'

'Anything reasonable,' said Dawlish.

'Will you undertake to surrender Bland to us?'

'Provided it's possible. One hour with Bland is all I want.'

'Right,' said Trivett. 'It's yours.'

'Bless your heart,' said Dawlish. 'He's at Four Ways, and he asked me to go and see him after dark tonight. Before that, I want to look in at the hospital. Supposing you get your cordon in place at once? By the time the men are in position, I'll be there.'

Dawlish drove from The Pines soon afterwards, haunted by the suddenly faced possibility that Ted and Tim, while following Graham, had been trapped in the fire. He drove along the quiet country roads, passing very few people, aware that there was a very real chance that he would be attacked. Any hedge might hide one or more of the men who had carried out that fantastic raid at The Grange. Any tree stump might hide a gun.

He reached the hospital at last, and was taken to the small private ward, where Felicity lay, still drowsy from the anaesthetic. He sat with her for an allotted ten minutes, telling her nothing of what had happened.

He left the hospital with a strange feeling of anxiety and relief; relief that there was now no danger for Felicity, anxiety because he might never see her again. It was an odd feeling. He was not usually jumpy; in all his previous adventures he had taken it for granted that he would get through, but now—

He drove without incident along the narrow road until he reached the turning towards Four Ways. Parking the car in a convenient gateway, he switched off the lights, and stood looking about him for a few moments, to get his eyes used to the darkness. How long it seemed since he had first set eyes on the place, and he and Felicity had fallen in love with it!

Would they ever live there?

A dull light came from a downstairs window. Then suddenly a shadow passed across it.

Dawlish watched closely, hardly hearing his own breathing. There was no other sound. He went a little nearer, and stopped. That time he heard a sound, *behind him*.

So the house was being watched.

He walked on, keeping to the grass verge. If someone were immediately behind him, his own figure was a clear silhouette against the window. He felt on edge. A bullet might come out of the darkness at any moment. He reached a cluster of trees and drew out his gun, turning to face the direction from which he had come.

There was a faint movement, enough to verify that he had been followed. He waited, tensely, and then sharp and clear came the shrill cry of a night-jar, piercing the silence.

There was a pause, and then from further up the drive came an answering cry. The men who had made them, the one in front, and the one behind, were drawing nearer. He admired their stealth and their efficiency—and, at the very moment he judged they were about to leap on him, said pleasantly:

'No shooting, gentlemen, please.'

There was a muffled gasp, and then: 'Pat!'

'Well, well, well!' exclaimed Tim Jeremy. 'To think of all that masterly sleuthing being wasted on you!'

'How near you came to a bash on the head you'll never know!' gasped Ted.

'It's possible your own head might not have remained bash-less,' suggested Dawlish. 'However, I don't mind admitting I'm heartily relieved to see you both. I thought you had joined the funeral pyre. What brought you?'

'Graham is here, *en famille*,' said Ted.

'Meaning Marion and Belle?' asked Dawlish.

'Meaning just that. They came together. We *think* Bland is inside, too. Are you expecting any particular development?'

'Certainly I am,' declared Dawlish. 'No less than the final showdown. A declaration of principle by Algernon L. Bland, Esquire. The police have a cordon round the place at a discreet distance,' he added, 'and they're giving me one hour. There are also a dozen or so hearties belonging to the other side somewhere in the neighbourhood. Seen any signs of them?'

'No,' said Ted and Tim, in unison.

'Let's hope they've faded out,' said Dawlish, 'though I don't think it likely. I think you two had better stay at the doors, front and back. If there should be a sudden exodus, put a stop to it.'

'We'd probably do much better inside,' suggested Ted, hopefully.

'Not this time. Bland might be shy. If there's half a chance, I'll call you in.'

They accepted the charge without further protest, and walked softly up the drive. Dawlish gave them two minutes, and then stepped on to the porch.

He rang the bell.

Standing there in the silence it was hard to realise that Ted and Tim were within call, and that the police were not far away. He felt very much on his own—and he felt an odd reluctance to go through with it. Would Bland talk freely?

I'm crazy, he muttered to himself.

There was no sound, and his finger was on the bell-push again when the door opened. There was light in the hall from a door on the right—that charming room where he had met

Bland for the second time. He heard no voices, saw only Bland's advancing figure.

'I am *very* glad you have come, Dawlish,' he said quickly, '*very* glad indeed!'

He put out a hand and drew Dawlish in. Then he closed the door and switched on the hall light.

CHAPTER TWENTY-FOUR

BLAND PROPOSES

But for a minimum of furniture, the charming room was empty. The spirit of the Owens had gone.

That was a shock, and Dawlish felt an acute sense of disappointment as he looked about it.

'Sit down, my dear fellow,' said Bland. 'What will you drink?'

'Nothing, thanks,' said Dawlish.

'Oh, come! Let us be convivial! Major Dawlish—or may I call you Patrick?—I do not conceal from you the fact that I have met few people for whom I have such a high regard. You are aware that I am now hunted by the police?'

'Yes,' said Dawlish.

'And presumably you have arranged with the police to be outside,' said Bland, with a little chuckle. 'You see, I do not under-rate your intelligence! A whisky and soda, shall we say? Those excellent people, the Owens, left some behind—souls of hospitality, as I am sure you will agree. And'—Bland beamed— 'it is *not* poisoned!' He poured himself out a liberal measure of whisky, added soda, and then raised his glass. 'Ah, a rare stimulant, and one in which I seldom indulge, but this is an occasion.

Now, you are doubtless wondering when I am going to come to the point. I do not blame you! You are a man of action, with the added quality of a resourceful mind. You are doubtless expecting to pump me dry of all useful information, before the police close in.' He beamed. 'I am overconfident you think? But I have the best of reasons for that confidence, Major Dawlish, for I do not believe, when you know everything, you will allow the police to get me.

'You strike me as being a man with an unbiased mind,' Bland went on. 'And so I hope to convince you of the goodness of my cause. If I read you aright, Patrick, you are *above* the police, as I am. However, if I should fail to convince you, I still retain a means of persuasion.'

'Now you sound like business,' said Dawlish.

Bland beamed.

'I will elaborate. Graham, his daughter and the lady to whom he is engaged to be married, are in this house. I am an ingenious man, Patrick, and I have arranged a little trick. *If* you help me, all will be well. If you refuse, I will perform one little action, and, *hey presto*, off they will go into the next world!'

'Very original,' murmured Dawlish.

'Oh, I claim no originality,' said Bland. 'Those methods which have been well-tried are often better than novel ones. The point I wish to stress is that the lives of those three people are in your hands. You alone can save them. Shall we talk seriously?'

'It would seem to be a fairly sensible thing to do,' said Dawlish.

'Then do sit down, my dear fellow. Would you like a cushion? No. Very well, I will start.' Bland sat back in his chair and sipped his drink. He showed no fear whatever— and Dawlish was assured he felt none—that his plan would go awry. 'You know, of course, that *oil* in large quantities has been discovered in this district?'

'I know that some people think so,' said Dawlish.

'Oh, it is more than that! Perhaps you have asked yourself why, if it is here in such quantities, the Government did not operate wells during the war. The reason is simple. Oil, in the opinion of some people, has no commercial future in this country. Interested parties did not *want* oil, in substantial quantities, to be discovered here. Our friend Graham was one!' Bland laughed. 'Graham is a remarkable man in some ways. He was genuinely—you will find this hard to believe—horrified at the prospect of a gusher built at Hindhead. He considered it would be the ruin of the district. It would spoil the natural beauties. What a limited intelligence—don't you agree?'

'Unusual, certainly,' said Dawlish, drily.

'It was more remarkable because Graham, the owner of so much land, could have made a fortune. But he chose not to. He preferred penury. So, I set myself to make him change his mind. Shall I tell you *why*?'

'As soon as you like,' said Dawlish.

Time was flying, and he was already beginning to get uneasy about the police. Trivett would probably act within the hour, which put zero hour at a quarter to eleven; it was now ten o'clock.

'The reason is simple,' declared Bland. 'I spoke to you once before about my interest in men of bravery and valour so ill-rewarded by an ungrateful country. Do you know what I have done, Major Dawlish? I have decided to give four hundred of such men an *equal* share in the proceeds from the oil in this part of Surrey!

'You look surprised. I was afraid that you did not believe me when I talked on this subject before, but I am serious. Now, *this* is the situation. Graham, and a handful of others, do not wish the oil to be developed. The *truth*, of course, is that their interests are very deep in foreign oil and fuel companies!'

'I thought Graham—' began Dawlish.

'My dear young man, Graham is not wholly absolved from the motive of greed. He has recently become a great deal better off. Why? Because certain members of a syndicate, headed by a man called Justin, a wealthy coal owner, gave him shares in their companies if he would undertake *not* to sell The Grange. I, myself, have decided that the natural wealth of the country must not be denied the men who have earned, by their blood and by their heroism, the right to share in it. Unless I am gravely mistaken in you, Patrick, you share those sentiments.'

'Let's assume that I do,' said Dawlish.

'You are shy of admitting it, but I see your approval is there! Well, I set myself, with the aid of Perry Lamb, to weaken Graham's resistance. Much of this you know. I had some influence on Linda Keen's young brother. I used him to obtain the support of Graham's daughter. Unfortunately, he was attracted by her. It is *impossible* to reason with the emotions. That is a thing I gave up trying to do many years ago. Perhaps you have guessed that Keen, deeply in love with Marion, threatened to tell her the truth, as far as he knew it.'

'I have,' said Dawlish.

Bland leaned forward and patted his hand.

'Well, that failed. Belle also failed me. After the first shock, I bore her no umbrage. I am grieved, but not embittered. Her conquest of Graham was much more complete than I had any reason to suspect. It was a case,' he added, a little sadly, 'of being too thorough in my methods. However, further difficulties were created. *Lamb* was bribed by Justin to work against me. Lamb betrayed the fact that Barry Keen was known to Marion Graham. He told the men whom I had already instructed to silence Keen, to take him to Layer Street. You are curious about the reason?'

'Very,' said Dawlish.

'It is simple. Had Keen seen Marion then, he would have told her the whole truth. One of the things which helped us was the fact that Graham and his daughter, once very fond of each other, were estranged. Keen would have told her that her father's life was in danger, and that would have settled the estrangement, in Lamb's opinion. Moreover, by making a clean breast of some little aberrations from the legal norm, Keen would have put himself beyond *my* power. I once persuaded Keen to rob the Layer Street house. There, he found proof that Graham knew of the oil. You see how delicately I worked, and how Lamb sabotaged my efforts.

'Such treachery is hard to believe,' went on Bland. 'I tackled him about it. Alarmed, he went to see Justin, but Justin had already left Cardiff. Lamb, cornered, planned to blackmail Justin! Justin killed him.'

'I see,' said Dawlish.

'By then, Justin was himself alarmed. If his part in hushing up the untold wealth of this district were known, it would get him into considerable disrepute. He had played a very active part, actually stealing the surveyor's encouraging report, and substituted one much less encouraging. Lamb, however, got hold of the original. You see how everything worked out?'

Dawlish nodded.

'There were little odds and ends to tidy away,' said Bland. 'The unfortunate man who perished in the shed, for instance, could have betrayed Lamb; Lamb arranged his death. However, time is getting on, and I have no doubt that the police have a zero hour already fixed.' Bland looked up inquiringly, but Dawlish said nothing. 'I hope you will give me good warning. I should hate to think of those three people being killed unnecessarily.' Suddenly he stood up, stepped to the fireplace, and stood with his back to it. His voice deepened, losing all playfulness. 'Major Dawlish, listen to me! I shall not allow the police to take me alive. I have made sure of that. But my cause must live on. Once, I hoped that I would be able to take an open part in this. I can no longer hope for that. I can direct, but I must live in retirement. I want a man whom I can trust implicitly to carry out my plans, plans wholly for the benefit of others. Patrick, I want *you* to do this for me. It is strange that we began as adversaries, but always I have seen in you a kindred spirit. And I have cause for gratitude. It was *Justin* who fired at me from the grounds of The Pines, *Justin* who tried to kill you but, I am told, wounded your wife.'

A clock on the mantelpiece, behind Bland, pointed to twenty-five minutes past ten.

'Graham's part has been less heinous than Justin's,' Bland went on, 'As I do not propose that revenge be taken on him. He now has no reason to refuse to sell his land, for his house has gone.'

'Did you do that?' asked Dawlish.

'It was arranged at my suggestion,' said Bland, a little smugly. 'I needed some forces to help me in my mission, and so I enlisted a number of men, rather violent men, I agree, but good at heart. They carried out my instructions carefully. You see, Patrick, *nothing* can be allowed to stop me, I am something of a demogogue, I might say. *Well!*' His voice boomed out. 'There is the position. I want you to arrange for me to escape in safety. I want you to act for me in my many activities. I want you to feel that you are helping those many people who so richly deserve help. And incidentally,' added Bland, with a little smile, 'I want you to save the lives of the three other people in this house. Well, my dear Patrick. What is your answer?'

CHAPTER TWENTY-FIVE

DANGER!

Dawlish looked at the clock again, while Bland waited. It was twenty-five minutes to eleven. In ten minutes the police raid would begin.

In ten minutes Graham, Belle, and Marion might be dead.

The man in front of him was true to himself; grandiose motives, a kind of auto-hypnosis, backed up by threats. That he really proposed to make a fortune out of oil, Dawlish had no doubt at all. That he would, if the situation demanded it, throw aside the men whom he professed to regard so highly, was beyond all reasonable doubt. That he would feel confidence that Dawlish's agreement would give him a stranglehold was equally certain. He believed that Dawlish would play into his hands completely.

Bland said: 'When *are* the police due?'

'At eleven o'clock,' said Dawlish.

'Indeed. Then we have good time, my dear Patrick!'

Dawlish nodded. At least he was believed there; at a quarter to eleven, Bland would be taken completely by surprise. That might be helpful, but—*could* Bland ensure the death of the other three? The possibility haunted Dawlish.

How would he attempt it? At first Dawlish had thought that he had a switch or press-button in his chair, to blow them up. Such an arrangement would be simple, but Bland had now moved to the fireplace. Was the switch near there? Could he, by stretching out a hand, send them to eternity?

Or was it something which would happen if the door of their room were touched, or if windows were opened? Whatever it was, he had complete confidence, and Dawlish did not think he was bluffing.

'Time enough,' repeated Bland with a touch of irritation, 'but none to waste, my dear friend. And now, your answer?'

'It isn't a thing to decide in a moment,' said Dawlish.

'You have no choice,' snapped Bland. 'The decision must be made at once.'

The telephone bell rang in the hall.

To Dawlish, it brought immeasurable relief. *Where* were the Grahams and Belle? How could he make Bland tell him the truth about them? Would a threat of physical violence be of any use?

He followed Bland to the telephone.

'Yes,' he heard him say, 'speaking. How far away? A hundred yards. I see. What is that . . . . Are you sure? . . . *Thank* you.'

He replaced the receiver slowly. Dawlish slipped his hand into his pocket; the cold steel of the gun was comforting. Bland turned and faced him. The light in the hall was full on, every feature of the man's face made clear. He looked anguished, heart-broken; it was an incredible sight. When he spoke there was a sob in his voice.

He said: 'So you deceived me, Dawlish. The man whom I trusted with my life has deceived me. The police are already moving in. One of my men has telephoned to tell me so. Dawlish, the consequences of this betrayal will be frightful—frightful. *Not a man among the police will remain alive.* I have arranged that. Dawlish! *Put up your hands!'*

He stood there, apparently completely defenceless, yet the tone of his voice made Dawlish pause. It was an effort of will to take the automatic out of his pocket.

'*Put up your hands,*' Bland repeated, 'a man is on the stairs. If you move your gun again he will shoot you.'

Bluff, thought Dawlish. I—

The sneeze of a shot fired from a silenced gun was followed by the thud of a bullet in the wall by his side.

'You alone can get me out of this house safely,' Bland said in a thin voice. 'You must arrange it, Dawlish. Three people in this house are nearer to death at this moment than they have ever been. There are the police outside, and unless you save me from them, not one of them will remain alive!'

Dawlish said frigidly: 'I'm calling your bluff.'

'You—foolish—fellow' said Bland. The words sounded like a sigh. 'Dawlish, listen to me. Phosgene gas is in flimsy containers beneath the floors of every room, every landing, every passage in this house. The boards have partitions, tiny partitions, between them. It will seep through them, through the wainscotings, through every tiny aperture. All men who step into this house and all men who are in it will be killed, Dawlish, do you understand? *I* may go with the rest of them, but—'

Dawlish said: 'I'm calling your bluff, Bland.'

'There *is* no bluff!' screamed Bland. 'Don't stand there like a fool, get me away from here! There is no bluff, I intend to carry it out, I shall—'

The door flew open with a crash. Dawlish saw Tim leaping into the room, springing at Bland—and he saw Tim suddenly crumple up, winged by a bullet fired from the silenced gun. Bland screamed hideously:

'*Release the gas, release the gas, release the gas!*'

A cold, unemotional voice spoke from the landing.

'They can't do it,' it said.

Graham stood there, dishevelled and unarmed. He began to come downstairs, limping as if he were injured.

'I got free, Bland.' He looked at his enemy, who was staring wild-eyed upwards, his eyes glaring, his mouth open.

'Dawlish,' said Graham, 'don't bring too many men into this house, pressure on certain parts of the floors might release the gas. Oh, it is there, right enough, he has not lied.' He was breathing heavily, and coming down the stairs one at a time, every step an effort. 'Keep Bland,' he added, 'we have not heard the last of his crimes yet. Don't let him—'

He stopped abruptly.

'*Bland!*'

Dawlish, half-turning, saw the Mills bomb in the man's hand. Dawlish leapt at him, moving swiftly enough to seize the thing, *but the pin was drawn*. Gripping it lightly, Dawlish ran towards the open door. He saw the headlights of cars suddenly break the darkness, and the moving figures of Trivett's men not far down the drive. With all his strength he flung the bomb away from him, praying that it would not injure any of the approaching men. One of them, suddenly illuminated in the headlamps, seemed to realise his danger and flung himself down.

The bomb exploded.

The blast struck Dawlish like a physical blow, as he staggered towards Trivett, now appearing from the back door.

'Stay there,' Dawlish cried in a tense voice. 'Don't let your men in, Bill, don't let them in.'

The tone of his voice and the expression on his face was enough to check Trivett, who stood indecisively by the door, watching, as if mesmerised, the mêlée of struggling men.

He said hoarsely: 'Right, Pat!'

Graham, dishevelled, injured, rose from Bland's unconscious body.

'Where is Marion? She and Belle are in this house somewhere!' He looked at Dawlish with glazed eyes. 'Find her, find her before the gas is released!'

In Dawlish's imagination, he could already see the faint mist of the gas rising up from the floor. He turned to Trivett.

'Have your men got gas masks?'

'No,' said Trivett. 'I—'

'Send for some,' said Dawlish sharply. He pointed to Ted's inert figure, by whom Tim was standing. 'Off you go, Tim,' he said, 'every one of you who can walk, or are capable of carrying those who can't. This is my job.'

It was very quiet. Dawlish found himself looking searchingly at the floorboards. They were of good quality, and the joints seemed sealed, but he knew better than to rely on that.

He looked in each of the downstair rooms.

When he came back from his fruitless quest, Tim was back and Trivett was standing by him. Trivett's voice came quietly.

'Talk of gas is probably a bluff.'

'Don't you believe it,' said Dawlish. He watched while Trivett took a pair of slim, modern handcuffs from his pocket, and fastened Bland's right wrist to a bannister bar. Then they started up the stairs, Dawlish leading the way, knowing that one false step might release the gas. Tense, rigid, they reached the first landing. Six doors were in sight; three were standing open.

The rooms with the open doors were empty.

Dawlish saw Trivett and Tim reach a closed door and open it; and then another; nothing happened. He turned the handle of the sixth door, the last in sight.

The door was locked.

He stood still for a moment, and the others joined him. He did not know what might happen when he forced the door. It might release gas, or explosive.

'Use a key,' said Trivett in a sharp voice. He took out a skeleton key, and handed it over.

Dawlish slipped it into the keyhole. The lock looked simple enough, but there was no welcome click. The key would not work. Trivett shouldered him roughly aside, and tried; he had no better luck.

Dawlish tapped on the door; softly at first, then louder. It brought a reward, for Marion's voice responded.

'Who is there?'

'Dawlish! Can you—'

'Be careful!' she cried. 'Don't try to come in, don't force the door. It will release gas if you do. There's only one way to get us out.'

'Which way?' Dawlish demanded.

'By the ceiling,' she said. There was a moment's pause, and then she added: 'For God's sake tread carefully. The house is mined. Any touch, any pressure, and the gas will be released.'

Dawlish said: 'When you hear a tap on the ceiling, tap back, do you understand?'

'Yes.'

'Are you alone?' Dawlish asked.

'Belle is here,' said Marion. 'She's gagged. Hurry! Hurry!'

Hurry, thought Dawlish.

He turned and led the way towards the bathroom; there he had seen a loft, with a patent ladder resting against the wall, He trod lightly, and yet his feet seemed leaden. Disaster seemed to hover about them, a thing which they might bring on themselves at any moment. He was tall enough to move the loft covering to one side. Trivett put the ladder into position, and Dawlish climbed up.

With infinite patience he wriggled into the loft. The light from the bathroom showed him the gaunt wooden timbers of the roof. He pressed a switch at the side of the cover, and a single, unshaded bulb lit up. Then he glanced downwards.

There, in front of him, was a series of small glass containers. There were others, dotted about the loft; too many to move easily without touching them. He went down on his knees and lifted the deadly things one by one, making a path towards the floor above the room, where the women were incarcerated. He could not get the layout of the place clear in his mind's eye. Which *was* the room?

HURRY, HURRY!

Trivett joined him. They did not dare to move right or left. Suddenly a faint tapping came ahead of them.

Dawlish reached the spot, judged the position of the room, and tapped with his knuckles. There was an answering knock— too loud, far too loud; a phial jumped.

'All right!' he cried, and turned to Trivett. 'Bill, for God's sake move these things away as carefully as you know how!'

He took a large pen-knife from his pocket as he spoke, and began to prise at the floorboards immediately over the room. One after another he turned the screws, took them out, and laid them gently on one side. Tim and Trivett were working with the phials. Once or twice he heard the chink of glass.

He moved one board; a second, and a third.

Beneath them were joists.

He worked the knife into the plaster, twisted right and left, and small pieces came away. These he put carefully on one side. He could see Belle and Marion. Belle was now free from the gag.

He had the hole large enough at last.

Trivett joined him. Dawlish called to Marion, and gave her instructions. She pulled a chair beneath the hole, then turned to Belle.

'You go first,' she said.

'No,' said Belle, 'I—'

'Don't waste time!' cried Dawlish.

Marion stood on the chair and stretched her arms upwards. He took her wrists and pulled, his muscles strained to the utmost. She came up slowly, until at last she was able to grip the floorboard which had not been moved.

'Now we won't be long,' said Dawlish. 'I—'

A sound made him stop. It was not in the loft, but he thought it came from the first floor.

It was the sound of breaking glass!

CHAPTER TWENTY-SIX

BROKEN GLASS

Marion's hand slipped.

Dawlish clutched her wrist and saved her from falling.

Trivett said: 'I'd better go. Hold on to him, Tim.'

He went off, while Dawlish began to think more clearly. The gas might rise a little, but not enough to be immediately effective. There was time enough, if he were reasonably quick and careful.

'Tim,' he said, as he began to haul Belle inch by inch through the gap, 'get down, find out where it's broken. Open all windows, and make a note of the nearest one it is possible to climb out of.'

Trivett was talking downstairs; that was a good sign, thought Dawlish. He turned to Marion. Her face was dead white, the red marks at her mouth showing up like whip lashes.

'Gently does it,' he muttered. 'Crawl to the ladder, follow Tim, and do what he tells you.'

'But Belle—'

'I'll look after Belle,' said Dawlish.

Marion began to crawl away, and he renewed his pull on Belle. She was a much heavier woman than Marion and there was more than a chance that he would not be able to get her through the gap.

Up, up—pause—up, up—pause.

Ten seconds, twenty, and his arms were nearly pulled from their sockets. Then she was beside him.

He lay there, spent, motionless for a moment, the only sound his harsh, sobbing gasps.

Someone appeared above him—he did not recognise the face, for it was hidden by a gas mask. A muffled voice said: 'The woman's taken care of, and you're all right for a few minutes. No longer.' A hand reached out, got a grip on Dawlish's elbow, and helped him up.

'Bathroom,' said the other; it was Trivett.

Dawlish went down the loft ladder, hardly daring to think. No one else was in the room, he saw no one in the passage outside. The window was wide open and the top of the ladder rested against it. Cars had been brought round to the side of the house, their headlamps full on. Dawlish went down, backwards, breathing in great gulps of air.

'I don't think much is released,' Trivett said, behind him.

'What happened?'

'Graham came back, and there was another fight with Bland. There was a small container we hadn't seen, near Bland's head, just beneath the carpet.'

'So Bland's dead?'

'I'm afraid he is. It's chlorine all right.'

'What about Graham?'

'He didn't stay long enough to be affected,' said Trivett. 'Did Bland talk?'

'He certainly did, though I don't know how much was true.'

'We'll soon winnow out the fact from the fiction,' Trivett said encouragingly.

A wide cordon had been put round the house, while a squad of men, in service masks, were on their way to clear the place up. Dawlish felt little or no interest in the proceedings. Bland had died; it was hard to realise that the colourful grandiose man with his warped philanthropy had gone, that Marion and Belle were safe, and that it was all over. Impossible to believe that they knew everything.

'Because we don't,' Dawlish muttered to himself.

He was taken to The Pines in a police car, and he was asleep within a minute of getting into bed. The whole affair had taken more out of him than he realised. Ted and Tim were in hospital, but their wounds were not serious. Trivett and Hall had taken the two women and Graham away, to a hotel in Haslemere. Dawlish knew all of these things, and yet they did nothing to relieve his feeling that there was still something wrong, badly wrong.

It remained with him when he woke up the next morning, and was still there when Trivett arrived. Trivett himself appeared strangely glum as he followed Dawlish into the drawing-room. It was some minutes before he spoke.

'Well, what about Bland's story?'

'Ah, yes,' said Dawlish. 'I'd better give you that.'

It was vivid in his mind, and it seemed to answer everything, but he could see that Trivett was a long way from satisfied. When he had finished, Trivett said:

'Pat, something is badly wrong. Justin had nothing to do with it. I've seen Barry Keen again. He's told me that Lamb and Bland, when talking together, arranged that Justin *should* be framed. The reason is fairly obvious. Bland had shares in Justin's colliery. He wanted to get a controlling interest, and Justin prevented him. However—Justin wasn't in this business. He had a water-tight alibi, and couldn't possibly have killed Lamb. Nor did he shoot at you. Lamb lied about him. There isn't any doubt about it,' he added. 'Justin *isn't* the man.'

'I'm not really surprised,' said Dawlish. 'Well, what next?'

'There's something which will mean bad news for Harcourt and his girl,' said Trivett, abruptly.

'Why them, in particular?'

Trivett said: 'Pat, there's no oil worth drilling for, in, or near The Pines. There just isn't! The surveyor's report which had such a glowing account was faked.'

Dawlish stared. 'Are you *sure*?'

'I'm quite sure. There were traces of oil. The Pines was taken over, and drillings were made. The results were negligible. All this business has been over nothing. Faked reports,' he repeated. 'Bland didn't know it, of course. Nor did Lamb. Someone did.'

Dawlish said: 'I wonder if—'

He stopped abruptly.

'Now I've got it! Bill, *Graham's our man!* Graham wanted to make a good profit on his land, Graham faked the report, got in touch with Lamb and Bland through a third party, got them interested in the land, and, when they approached him to sell, refused, so as to force the price up. All the time he pretended to be against selling, but he was only planning to get the highest bid.'

'But Graham—' began Trivett.

'Graham knew that Bland was suspicious,' said Dawlish. 'Graham is tall and thin, and answers the description of the man who tried to shoot me, who tried to shoot Bland, and who actually murdered Lamb. If Lamb and Bland were aware of the fraud, by then, he would have good reason to want them out of the way.'

'If—' began Trivett.

'There can't be any "if"!' roared Dawlish. 'There isn't anyone else who answers everything so well as Graham does. He has acted out of character from the very beginning. An aloof, rather arrogant man, who—Bill, Bill, I should never have been taken in by his acting. I could never really understand why he fell so heavily for Belle. She wasn't the type he would marry. I don't believe he intended to marry her, he just succeeded in beating Bland by encouraging her, by enlisting her on his side. Oh, he fits in everywhere! He got free when he was supposed to be helpless in Four Ways yesterday—'

'He says that he was in a different room from the others, but escaped,' said Trivett, dazedly. 'He—'

'Escape fiddlesticks! Bland finally got to the truth, and put it to Graham. He admitted it. First and last, they wanted money. They patched up a last minute collaboration. Neither, in the end, was strong enough to stand alone. Bland sent for me, hoping he could hoodwink me into letting him go, and acting as his stooge. The thing that mattered was to get names of reputable people not only on the board of Merrick Company, but on the board of the company which would take over The Grange estate. With that, plus the talk about oil, shares would go sky-high. Huge money would change hands. It was a gigantic fraud, and—'

'Now just a moment,' said Trivett. 'Graham loved The Grange too much to allow it to be burned down.'

'He didn't do that. Bland did. It was Bland's last act of revenge on the man. Bill, a dozen men or more were in the vaults at The Grange. How on earth did it ever seem reasonable that *Graham* knew nothing about them—'

'But they knocked out the staff and police!'

'You'll find they were bribed by Bland into turning on Graham,' said Dawlish. 'Have you found any of them?'

'I think we've picked up one or two,' said Trivett. 'Young Keen was able to tell us an address where they often gathered, and we've had men waiting for them.'

'Once you tackle 'em, you'll find I'm not far wrong,' said Dawlish. 'Oh, it's beautifully simple. Bland, completely hoodwinked, and then discovering that the story of oil had been put up simply to get him and others interested. Finally, after The Grange had gone—what a fiendish act of vengeance on Bland's part—Bland put an offer to Graham. "We must bury the hatchet and work together. We can still make a fortune. We must get Dawlish to help us—he has influence with the police." Can't you see it? And once he had Graham at Four Ways, he forced his hand, because he locked Marion and Belle up, after he had made the place lousy with gas. Graham wasn't finished, though. He bribed the men who were still working for Bland at Four Ways. He decided to rat on Bland. He did it well, too, pretending he'd fought his way free, though there was no sound of a struggle. He must have *been* free. He knew that only Bland was left to betray him. He had to kill Bland. He had the small phial of chlorine. He went in when the rest of the men outside were forbidden entry, smashed the phial near Bland's head, then told you Bland had come round. Bill, does it fit, or am I dreaming?'

'It *seems* to fit,' said Trivett. 'I—'

There was a shout from the passage—Harcourt's voice, raised in such alarm that Dawlish and Trivett swung round. The door was ajar. They caught a glimpse of Graham standing there, with a gun pointing towards them. But for Harcourt's cry they would not have had a moment's warning. As it was, Dawlish felt his heart turn over—

Graham fired, and missed.

Before he could fire again, Harcourt came tearing along the

passage. His chair, moving fast, was now a deadly weapon. It crashed into Graham and flung him violently against the wall.

'So that,' said Dawlish, 'is that.'

Graham made a full confession; nothing Dawlish had said was very wide of the mark, but there were small points which were cleared up. He had known for some time that Barry Keen was in Lamb's hands, and knew also that Bland was interested in oil. So he had worked through the youngster, to get at Bland and grip his interest. Then the battle between them had started. The main quarrel had been over Belle; a quarrel that brought the worst out of each man. One thing, too, which had puzzled Dawlish greatly, was the chlorine at Four Ways. That was Bland's doing; he had employed several men there for the two days the Owens had been away. He had planned that macabre poison chamber, knowing just where, in every room, the press of a switch would break the glass by exploding a small charge of dynamite. He had boasted about it to Graham.

'Yes,' Dawlish said, 'Bland believed in himself absolutely. He could not believe, even at the last, that Graham was going to beat him. Graham knew that if Bland were caught, he would probably tell the whole story.'

'You knew Bland better than I did,' said Trivett. 'You were wrong on one count, old chap—the fire at The Grange. It was Bland, of course—and Bland who got the men who were living in the vaults organised. Graham didn't know they were there. Bland wanted all the strong-arm men he could get. He told you he wanted to frame Graham, and that was true enough. Then when he decided to fire the place, he sent the men back to London. He kept only one of them—the one who was open to graft, and who helped Graham. Satisfied?'

'Yes,' said Dawlish, with a smile. 'More than satisfied.'

He was due to visit Felicity that afternoon, but before he left, Harcourt waylaid him. His face was wreathed in smiles, and the fact that the supposed fortune under The Pines was now non-existent, sat as lightly on his shoulders as on Linda's.

He grinned up at Dawlish.

'No, we don't want any boarders,' he said. 'We're going to manage here until we sell the place, and then get a bungalow. Oh, did I tell you that we're going to get married?'

Dawlish laughed.

'But my dear Simon, I could have told *you!* So it's wedding bells for you, and for Barry. Congratulations to you both, and long life and happiness to your beautiful brides.'

About this time an offer from an estate agent was made for The Pines. Harcourt closed the deal there and then, and later confided to Dawlish that he thought the purchaser must be mad.

'People are,' murmured Dawlish.

He wondered what he would do with the house. He certainly did not want it, although Bland's seven thousand pounds had been well spent in paying for it.

It was some weeks later, when Felicity was about again, and Tim and Ted were staying at Four Ways for a rest, that he received an inquiry about The Pines, which he had again placed on the market. It was ideally situated for a sanatorium for disabled men from the services.

Dawlish looked at Felicity. She nodded.

'Tell them they can have it as a gift,' said Dawlish.

'A—a gift!' stammered the agent.

'A gift,' said Dawlish, firmly, 'no strings attached.'

He told Felicity that it was odd, but he thought Bland would be pleased.

ABOUT THE AUTHOR

John Creasey, born in 1908, was a paramount English crime and science fiction writer who used myriad pseudonyms for more than six hundred novels. He founded the UK Crime Writers' Association in 1953. In 1962, his book *Gideon's Fire* received the Edgar Award for Best Novel from the Mystery Writers of America. Many of the characters featured in Creasey's titles became popular, including George Gideon of Scotland Yard, who was the basis for a subsequent television series and film. Creasey died in Salisbury, UK, in 1973.

THE PATRICK DAWLISH MYSTERIES

FROM OPEN ROAD MEDIA

EARLY BIRD BOOKS

FRESH DEALS, DELIVERED DAILY

Love to read?
Love great sales?

Get fantastic deals on bestselling ebooks delivered to your inbox every day!

Sign up today at
earlybirdbooks.com/book